Yes, we can !

J. TF.

20/8/88.

CAN I COUNT ON YOUR SUPPORT?

CAN I COUNT ON YOUR SUPPORT?

Canvassing Votes and Jokes

Foreword by The Prime Minister,
The Rt. Hon. JAMES HACKER

Compiled by
ROBIN CORBETT MP
and VAL HUDSON

Stanley Paul
London Melbourne Auckland Johannesburg

Stanley Paul & Co. Ltd

An imprint of Century Hutchinson Ltd
62–65 Chandos Place, London WC2N 4NW

Century Hutchinson Australia (Pty) Ltd
16–22 Church Street, Hawthorn, Melbourne, Victoria 3122

Century Hutchinson New Zealand Limited
PO Box 40–086, Glenfield, Auckland 10

Century Hutchinson South Africa (Pty) Ltd
PO Box 337, Bergvlei 2012, South Africa

First published 1986

Phototypeset by Input Typesetting Ltd, London SW19 8DR

Printed and bound in Great Britain by Anchor Brendon Ltd, Tiptree,
Essex

British Library Cataloguing in Publication Data

Can I count on your support?: canvassing
votes and jokes.
1. Elections—Great Britain—Anecdotes,
facetiae, satire, etc. 2. Campaign
management-—Great Britain—Anecdotes,
facetiae, satire, etc.
I. Corbett, Robin II. Hudson, Val
324.7   JN956

ISBN 0 09 166250 8

Contents

'What do you expect, with all the cut-backs in education?'

DEDICATION

We dedicate this book to all active, party canvassers – without whom politics would have far fewer funny stories.

May their souls never lose the ideals and passion which send them out, night after night – in all weathers – walking the streets of Britain in the name of democracy . . . and a pint in the pub afterwards.

THANKS . . .

. . . to all those who helped us with encouragement, inspiration, stories and cartoons.

. . . and to all who buy this book. All profits are going to The Save The Children Fund. They hope to raise enough money from this book to provide clean water for two villages in Papua New Guinea, where infant mortality is high. As a Council member for Save The Children, I thank you for *your* support.

ROBIN CORBETT MP

THE CANVASSER'S MOTTO

IF IT MOVES, CANVASS IT.
IF IT DOESN'T, STICK A POSTER ON IT.

A CANVASSER'S PRAYER

Dear Great Leader in the Sky . . . preserve, I beseech thee, my belief in my cause when my feet ache, the rain drippeth down my collar . . . and my canvass cards receive more 'Againsts' than 'Fors'.

I pray, Oh Leader, for thicker skin, stronger knees and tougher toes. May the nineteen smile muscles of my face never tire. May my canvass cards get ever more waterproof and may they never get jumbled up or worse, get lost. Make thou my pen not give up after the second call with 185 to go and may the doorbell always be answered. I pray for the wisdom to spot when 'I've already been to vote' is a fib – and when a 'Doubtful' is really a nice 'Against'.

Dear Leader, I am weary and hungry . . . let the 200 more doors to knock before I can go home, melt into one and above all, Oh Leader, please postpone tomorrow's polling day.

Foreword

The Rt. Hon. James Hacker PC MP B Sc (Econ).
Prime Minister and First Lord of the Treasury

I am delighted to be asked to write a foreword to this book. The aims of The Save The Children Fund have always been particularly close to my heart, and this has nothing to do with any considerations of improving my public image by associating myself with caring and compassionate causes. Nor is it motivated by any desire to minimize the damage to my electoral chances by the regrettable cuts we have recently been compelled to make in the welfare services.

It is also my hope that this book will help the cause of politicians generally. It is a sad fact of public life that so many people have been misled by the media into thinking of MPs as self-seeking, self-important windbags obsessed with their career ambitions, consumed with personal vanity, and fraudulently professing high principles which they are prepared to abandon instantly if they see them threatening their chances of re-election. This book will go some way to showing us in our true light as diffident, humble, almost saintly men and women concerned only with the good of others, and who make endless sacrifices with no thought of personal publicity, solely to try and create a better world for our fellow citizens and for the human race.

JAMES HACKER
No. 10 Downing St. SW1A 2AA

Introduction

There are just three groups of people who get excited at the approach of an election: the candidate, the party workers – and the punters. (Ladbrokes' biggest turnover is not at the Derby but at General Elections.)

For the rest of the country, initial media-stimulated interest as the date is announced soon shades off into something approaching apathy not to say sheer indifference . . . that is until the canvassing zealots race up the steps two at a time and pound the front door like a team from *The Sweeney*.

Canvassing and campaigning is all about getting a message across face-to-face (or mouth to ear . . . you could call it political resuscitation) and finding out where the support is, ready for the Big Day.

Most people like to be canvassed since they do not feel compelled to vote if no one bothers to ask them personally to do so. According to party activists, voters like – and expect – to be courted . . . even if it is by the wrong party. Great is the indignation of those who feel neglected: 'What? Vote for you lot when you never even called in on our Auntie Muriel last year after she'd walked all the way to the school to vote for you the year before? Not on your nelly.'

However, some voters would rather you extracted their teeth without anaesthetic than admit their political preference. Citizens who appear on national television to talk about their sex lives or how much they earn, can act like key-less sardine cans when discussing where they place the X on the ballot paper. Others can look you straight in the face – and lie about whom they support, while quite a few voters want to discuss their own troubles (it was noted that Marje Proops covered far fewer houses when she canvassed, than others in her 'team').

Apart from voters, other obstacles await the unwary . . . finding the wretched doorbell for example – people put them in the strangest places. And a few homes either do not have letter-boxes or have such snappy ones that you end the day without the tips of your fingers.

Canvassers have to contend with doors falling on their heads, lavatories cracking under them and babies wetting on them. They have been locked out, locked in, sprayed with a water hose and chased by a lawn mower. Their hands, through letterboxes, have been attacked by high-flying cats and their ankles bitten by dogs who weren't supposed to hurt a flea. False teeth, glass eyes, a faulty cistern, pythons, skunks and many nude women all loom large in their memories, as this book will show.

And we haven't yet got to the Big Day.

When D-Day dawns (always a Thursday, no one knows why), it then becomes a matter of shoe-horning promised supporters out of their homes into the polling stations by persistent, cajoling, recklessly promising canvassers, determined to get the maximum number out to vote before 10 pm on election night.

It is not always easy. British inventiveness is at its most imaginative on polling day, whether at a general, local or by-election. Whole streets of voters are 'waiting for my husband/wife to come back from work'; 'just finishing tea'; 'bathing the baby'; or 'will vote after *Coronation Street/EastEnders/Dallasty*'.

Some will not vote whatever happens, like religious sectarians who refuse to vote in earthly elections though they take full advantage of earthly schools, water, police and roads. Some even boast that they have never ever voted – do they realize that 'Bad politicians are elected by good citizens who do not vote'? Quite a few don't vote because 'all politicians are the same' (they're not, they're not).

Sometimes – though not often – there's truth in the apparent excuse. One senior MP tells how a man shouted through his kitchen window that he couldn't vote because his foot was caught in an electric mangle. He had slipped while painting a ceiling. Freed by Labour canvassers and taken to vote, he said proudly on the way back, 'That's the first time I've ever voted.' Then, as an after-thought: 'And I voted Conservative.'

A Birmingham councillor tells how a woman refused to vote because she couldn't find her false teeth. 'Here,' he said, putting his hand to his mouth, 'borrow these.'

You need that kind of nimble wit and determination to succeed on the doorstep. But enthusiasm is not enough. A canvasser is part of a national sales force usually with no more than a few minutes to describe the product, praise its plus points and go for the 'sale'. The way you dress, speak, listen and respond can be critical to whether you convert – or believe you have.

Old hands on the knocker tell tales of people who for years have said 'Yes' to whichever party calls, just as canvass records show years of seeming 'Don't Know' indecision by around one elector in five. Same people, but are they the same 'doubts', or are they updated as candidates and parties change?

Yet that's what canvassing is all about: to silence doubt, to strengthen belief or to undermine convictions which promise a vote against your candidate. People either love or loathe canvassing. The lovers would do it on Christmas Day but for prudence. We call activists who hate canvassing 'Scarlett O'Haras'. They all believe 'tomorrow is another day'.

The rule is simple: if you don't like it, don't do it. The fact that you are uncomfortable will show. The trick is to team up with an experienced friend and give it a go. Otherwise this will be the first and last edition of *Can I Count On Your Support?*

Robin Corbett MP
Val Hudson

Westminster, June 1986

1
There's Nowt so Queer as Voters

NEIL KINNOCK MP

Labour canvassers calling at a mansion in an insuperably Tory part of Surrey are traditionally met by the butler who takes their manifesto on a silver tray to the Duchess. Her Ladyship then provides heart-warming whisky and the information that she is a socialist who sadly cannot vote but the butler, gardener, cook and maids are all Conservatives who sadly can.

J S SCRUTON (activist)

During a local council election in North Hull, it was nearly dusk and I was about to finish for the evening when I knocked at a door in a side street. It was opened by an elderly man. I explained the purpose of the call to which he responded with a 'Well, I'd like to know a bit more about this but the missus and I are just getting ready for bed.'

I offered to call again another time but he insisted that I enter the house. 'Come upstairs,' he said and I followed him up to the bedroom, where his wife was already partially undressed. 'Carry on talking,' he commanded – 'as long as you don't mind our getting on and into bed. We like to go to bed early.'

So I did and by the time I'd finished, they were both undressed and in bed. They both thanked me, said they thought my candidate would get both their votes (which, I checked later, he did) and asked me if I'd kindly switch off the light and drop the latch on the front door as I went out. They were such a pleasant, friendly couple, I almost felt tempted to tuck them up before I left!

GLENDA JACKSON

I heard of an incident some years ago when one of the Sainsbury brothers was canvassing as a prospective Parliamentary candidate. He knocked on a door, introduced himself and received a tirade from the household to the effect that Sainsburys had put the charges for their carrier bags up to fourpence.

PETER WALKER MP

I was canvassing as the Conservative candidate for Dartmouth in the 1955 General Election. I called at one house where the lady hushed me to be quiet when I introduced myself as Peter Walker, the Conservative candidate. I thought I must have woken a baby and perhaps another vote was lost. Quietly she whispered to me, 'My old man's Labour and I've told him Polling Day is on Friday!'

JEFFREY ARCHER

As a young MP at the time of decimalization, I was worried that some old age pensioners might not fully understand what the changes meant. One Saturday morning, I went to the local Safeways to check how it was working out. One old lady was having tremendous trouble remembering that there used to be 240 pennies in the pound and that there were now only 100 pennies. I went up to her and tried to help and explain why the Government had brought the measure in. She looked me straight in the eye and said, 'Don't you worry my friend, it will never catch on.'

KEVIN McNAMARA MP

During my canvassing, I knocked on one door and said, 'Hello, I'm from the Labour Party.' The man looked puzzled and capped his ear in his hand: 'Eh?' I tried several times more with the same response then gave up smiling: 'OK, thank you.' Just as I was approaching the garden gate, the man shouted: 'Don't forget to shut the gate.'

'Bugger the gate,' I retorted, believing he wouldn't hear.

'And bugger the Labour Party,' he shouted back.

ANONYMOUS MP

7.30pm   Call on constituent with problem. Asked in by attractive female and offered drink.

7.40pm   Attractive constituent cannot find any drink and 'pops out for a second' to get something.

8.00pm   Constituent still away so leave note to say I cannot wait and will call again.

8.05pm   Find front door is locked with mortice lock.

8.10pm   Find all windows and exits are barred.

8.15pm   Use constituent's phone to explain to family why not able to be home as arranged.

11.15pm   Constituent returns home from pub with gaggle of friends to look at captive parliamentary candidate.

11.30pm   Candidate returns home to find door bolted and family gone to bed in disgust.

JONATHAN SAYEED MP

I was visiting constituents' homes after the '83 General Election, and I knocked on one door which was opened by an elderly lady with pebble glasses, and that quizzical expression which often denotes deafness. Speaking slowly and clearly, I said to her 'Good morning, madam, I am Jonathan Sayeed, your new Member of Parliament'.

'Oh, Mr Benn,' she replied, 'you don't look half as daft as they say'.

TONY CARR-GOMM (Councillor)

Answers on the doorsteps of voters in West London to the question 'Can I count on your support?':

1. (Quite fierce) 'Yes, because you knocked on my door reasonably. The other lot last night knocked so loud, they woke the baby.'
2. (Very slow) 'No . . . no . . . I don't vote much these days.'
3. (Eventually and cheerfully after I realized he was very deaf, my fortissimo was rewarded with): 'It's all right, thank you. They brought me half a hundredweight yesterday and promised me half a hundredweight next week.'

JOHN MAXTON MP

I knocked the door, introduced myself and asked the man whether he'd be voting Labour. 'That's none of your bloody business,' he told me.

'Well, you don't have to tell me,' I said casually. 'It just helps us to know where our support is.' Then noticing his splendid rose display, I commented on it. That got him going. He stopped short and said; 'I never vote Tory. Can't stand that little s--t the MP.' I smiled.

He talked on about his roses, then added; 'Never vote SNP, either. Independence for Scotland? It's mad.' Having nailed him down thus far, I went in for the kill. 'So does that mean you'll be voting for me then?' adding, as a reckless after-thought; 'Or will it be Liberal?'

'Oh there's a Liberal candidate, is there?' he asked, looking pleasantly surprised. 'I'll probably do that then.' Scanning the horizon for a swarm of aphids, I put him down as 'doubtful'.

JEANNE CAESAR (PS to Bob McTaggart MP)

On the day of the first 1974 General Election I 'knocked up' an elderly Labour supporter with an offer of transport. His daughter answered their door dressed in mourning and said 'I am so sorry, love, Dad passed away two days ago and so can't get out to vote.' She went on to explain that when she knew her father was dying she tried to rally him by shaking a newspaper over him which said that Heath might get re-elected, 'So you must get up to vote Labour on Thursday', but her father was 'too far gone'.

ARTHUR GROVES (agent, Lab)

Somewhere in the Midlands is a man with a guilty secret. Throughout the 38-year marriage of this Labour supporter he and his Tory wife have 'never voted'. They made a pact on their wedding day that politics would never rear its ugly head in their household. His wife has faithfully stuck to her promise. But every election day since they wed, the man has, during the early evening, gone to the library to 'exchange his books'. Which he does . . . on the way back from the polling station. So the husband is red rather than well-read, and the wife is Labouring under a misapprehension.

TIM SAINSBURY MP

The second election in 1974 was, for the three of us who had contested the by-election in November 1973, (Alex Fletcher, Alan Beith and myself) the third in less than a year. So I understood the attitude of the housewife responding to the canvassers who called on her: 'Not this week, thank you.'

PAT JOLLY (former Labour Party agent)

When Jack (now Lord) Diamond was standing in a Gloucester by-election, a young couple told my wife and I that they couldn't vote as they had a young baby. 'No problem,' said I. 'My wife's a qualified nurse. We'll take care of the baby till you get back.'

That was 8.30 pm and they didn't come back till 7 am the next day. 'Oh,' they told us, 'we had a bit of a go on the Labour. Would you like a cup of tea?'

W. J. GRIFFITHS MEP

Canvassing in the town of Barry one afternoon I knocked on a door which was answered by an old lady. I explained to her that

I was calling on behalf of Darwin Hinds the Labour candidate in the by-election and I hoped that she would be able to give him her support on polling day. She replied that she most certainly would because, when Mayor, he had spoken at a meeting she attended and she knew him to be a wonderful Christian gentleman. I must admit that I did not dissent, though the late Mr Hinds had been the first black Muslim mayor in Britain.

PATRICK CORMACK MP (Cons)

I was seeking to unseat the Labour candidate in one of the safest Labour wards in Grimsby in 1961 and had to bang fairly hard on the first door in a long row of rather drab terrace houses. At long last a large unshaven gentleman appeared with open shirt and no collar, broad braces and an intriguing tatoo on his chest. At least what bit I saw made it look rather intriguing to the virgin canvasser.

'Yes', he growled, somewhat to my surprise, 'You can count on my support young man if you will do something for me'. I was apprehensively eager to oblige. 'You get the ruddy gravel out of my back passage and I'll vote for you.' With that he propelled me down the side of the terrace and pointed with anger to a back door he couldn't enter. I gather that a phone call to the council did the trick but I still have my doubts that gravelling for his vote did any good – particularly as there was a 'Vote Labour' sticker in his window.

TAM DALYELL MP

On a wet Thursday night, canvassing in Orangetown during a parliamentary by-election, myself and the prospective Labour candidate, Harry Ewing, were told: 'Mr Dalyell, I have already been to vote for Mr Ewing.'

'Are you sure?' I said. 'You've been to vote?'

'Yes,' he said, leaning on his front door, 'and my wife and her mother also went to vote for Mr Ewing down at the polling station.'

Well, the election was not that Thursday but a fortnight later. Harry and I, each of us with one leg now slightly longer than the other, limped away into the night.

J. S. SCRUTON (activist)

Experience has convinced me that a sizeable proportion of the population still does not realize the significance of a large coloured rosette. Even when wearing one and knocking on doors at election time, and before I have had the chance to open my mouth to start my canvassing spiel, I have at different times been mistaken for the rent collector, insurance man, sanitary inspector, the doctor, electrician come to fix the telly and the man who collects the money for the Sunday papers.

Most gratifying, however, was the occasion when, resplendent in my rosette, I was warmly welcomed into the house by a fond mother, under the impression that I was 'our Mary's new young man'. (I was over 40 at the time.) But as Mary herself wasn't in, I never had the opportunity to judge whether the description was a compliment or an insult.

BOB EDWARDS MP

A parliamentary canvasser asked the lady who came to the door whether he could see her husband about his voting intentions. 'No,' said the lady, 'I'm afraid it is impossible for you to see him. I am mending his one and only pair of trousers.' Under the circumstances we didn't have a leg to stand on.

JOHN HOME ROBERTSON MP (Lab)

Visiting an Orange Club, I was told: 'There is a rumour that you are a Catholic.'

'I am a Catholic.'

'Oh well, at least you're honest about it.'

A little later I met a lady in the street. 'Oh dear, I'm afraid I can't vote Labour much as I'd like to – I was the Conservative candidate's nanny.'

IAN MIKARDO MP (Lab)

During my fourteen years as Member of Parliament in Reading we had a card-index of all the electors with a separate card for each of them: Labour voters on white cards, Conservatives on blue, Liberals on pink, doubtfuls on buff, and people we had not yet contacted on green.

During the 1955 election campaign I was canvassing in East Ward and came across a house with three cards: Arthur Hunt on blue, Elizabeth Hunt on blue and Laura Hunt on green. I was not at all interested in talking to the first two, but knocked at the door in the hope of seeing Laura in order to sound her out.

The door was opened by a large bristly man, obviously Arthur Hunt, and I asked him if I could see Laura, and he said no she was away but would be back on Saturday. I thanked him, said good afternoon and was on my way to the garden gate and the street when he called me back.

'I know who you are,' he said *fortissimo* and *con spirito*, 'and I suppose you have come to ask me how I am going to vote. But I am not going to tell you. I have voted in every election since 1918, and I have never told anyone beforehand how I was going to vote and I have never told anyone afterwards how I voted.'

I was just a shade resentful, since I had studiously *not* asked him about his vote; and then an imp of mischief descended on me and I said: 'Well, that is surprising because I happen to know that the Conservatives have got you down as a regular Tory voter.'

The man-who-never-told turned purple. He spluttered and shouted 'Who the hell told them that? I've always voted Labour.'

HUGH McCALLION (Birmingham City Councillor)

Some of my funniest experiences were as chairman of the housing committee. People who are not accustomed to writing letters tend to use a kind of 'psychological vernacular' and this produces some colourful results.

A young couple who had lived for some time in a bed sitting room were desperate to get out. Part of the letter read: 'We are very keen to start a family but our position is hopeless. Can you please advise?'

An elderly lady living alone in a family house asked to have her gardens done. For some reason the men did the back but not the front. Some weeks later she wrote: 'Your men did a lovely job on my back but my front's still in a mess.'

An old chap in a ground floor maisonette wrote complaining about a noisy neighbour on the floor above: 'Can you do something about this woman on top of me – she's banging from morning to night.'

Finally a Treasurer's Report was referring to a proposal to

employ a social worker for the mentally ill. One paragraph put
an entirely different slant on it when it described: 'The elderly
mentally infirm social worker.'

Hitting the canvas

(Punch, 2 May 1979)

In the red corner, GUY PIERCE
Deep within the bowels of Ruskin House, epicentre of Croydon Central
Labour Party's nerve control, set on pink alert to wrest the seat from
the Conservatives (majority 164), all is tense.

In the red corner, GUY PIERCE

Can we gain the day?
   The brooding silence is disturbed only by the click of slide rule,
pocket calculator and abacus. Party activists hurriedly bring in the
latest muttered word from the street. Grim smiles betray the
confidence we all feel.
   It has been a hard fought campaign, especially in the latter stages
but gut reaction tells each man that we've got it in the bag . . .
Brighton will blow out and Palace will be back in the First Division.
   But what of David White's chances of securing Croydon Central
(majority 164) from John Moore, the latest in that peculiar political
animal, the Tory 'Golden Boy', following soft in the footsteps of
Johnson-Smith and Heseltine?
   There were five of us due to go out 'under canvas', but one by one
they defected – two seduced by Kenny Everett and one under strict
instruction to stay in because the wife might need the car.
   Sorry, Vic, but come the revolution 'I was only obeying orders' will
get you nowhere but up against the nearest brick wall.

Conditions prevailed against a short sharp burst of political motivating in the wide open spaces of the Labour heartland of the Waddon Estate – the rain was coming down in stair rods. Martin Walker, at twenty-eight already a veteran of five elections past, led me through the curtains of rain to Frank's place, where the local ward secretary lives with only a parrot for company.

This creature (the parrot, not Frank) is said to be so vociferously left wing that he puts Keir Hardie (and his mynah bird) in the shade. Local legend has it that in the 1964 campaign, the local party, short of equipment and funds, shackled the parrot to the roof-rack of the candidate's 1100 and, driving around the constituency, let the parrot have his head.

It was only when the local residents' association threatened to slap an injunction on the bird that he was released from his mobile perch.

The news from Frank is good and bad.

The New Communist Party (a bloke called Charlie) has urged that his supporters vote Labour on May 3rd.

The bad news is that the *Sunday Express* has smeared White over the front page with accusations of being dedicated 'to the destruction of Parliamentary democracy through the eventual break-up of the Labour Party.' So much for keeping personalities out of it.

Steeling myself for a night of bitter confrontation, I take the electoral roll check-list for Chatsworth Road and head out for what is the nearest thing to bed-sit land that Croydon has to offer.

Things start off badly.

In vain I search for 248 Chatsworth Road. Has the renowned inefficiency of local Labour organisation struck again? Or worse. Could there have been a grand foul-up at Electoral Registrar level?

For ten minutes I anxiously pace through the easing drizzle. In desperation I hail Martin who coldly informs me that I've been looking at the electoral roll number; the addresses are on the right of the card. Well, to be fair it's been five years since I was last out.

The first few houses offer no response. It begins to look as though Labour will sweep in if we can only gain the 'Out' vote.

Shove a few 'David White was sorry you were out when we called' – not as sorry as Guy Pierce, looking for signs of life.

At last a door opens. Female mid-forties/comfortable.

'Good evening, I'm canvassing on behalf of the Labour Party.' Bedecked in red day-glo I've hardly dropped in from Smith Square. 'I was wondering whether we might count on your support?'

'Well, I've always voted Labour . . .' The hesitancy betrays the 'but'. 'But . . . I feel a woman ought to be given a chance.'

Should my hackles rise? Should I heed Jim's words and refrain from lowering the Great Debate to the level of gutter insults?

No. Not because of any political scruples, but because I'm not there to spend time on doorstep conversions – leave that to Jehovah's Avon Ladies. All I want is For/Against/Doubtful.

I put the question to her that she'd be in a bit of a quandary if Shirley Williams led the Labour Party against Thatcher. Yes, she concedes. So isn't the sex of the candidate irrelevant? No. I bid farewell, putting that one down to female illogicallity.

A few more letter boxes gobble up 'David White was sorry etc . . .'

My eyes are beginning to strain looking for badly-Biro'd names above doorbells. So far I have come across thirteen different bell tones. How much does a door-bell chime composer earn? I'll put that to the next punter; that'll set him thinking. Or not.

Can't find Old People's Home. Approach Gothic block. Door opened by young girl.

'I'm looking for the Old Peoples Home . . .'

'This is it. Please come in.'

I indicate the names on the list.

'He's departed.'

'Moved locally?' I ask.

Her eyes are downcast.

As I query each name her face becomes greyer. I make my excuses and leave.

Only two more to go.

My penultimate bell-ring is met with my most dramatic response yet. The door flies open and I'm confronted with a harridan in her late twenties. 'Trotskyist!' she cries before I can get a word out, brandishing a copy of the *Sunday Express*. 'It's all in here,' thrusting the paper under my nose. 'He's nothing but a Trotskyist.' My patience runs out. 'That's Trotskyite,' I reply, looking nervously around for a Mexican with an ice-pick. 'And he's not.' If there's one aspect of political non-thinking over the past few years that rankles, it is the debasement of political vocabulary and the emotive fear instilled in words like 'Marxist', 'Fascist', 'Trotskyite' etc. Before I have time to explain to her the fundamentals of left-wing theory and since when has an electoral platform demanding a £60 a week minimum wage and a 35-hour week led to the end of parliamentary democracy as we know it, the door is slammed in my face.

I enter 'doubtful' on the card.

Numb with fury, I move on next door.

The door is answered by a woman almost a clone of my previous encounter.

'Oh,' regarding me with some distaste, 'I suppose I've got to put up with this sort of thing until May 5th.'

Dear God, is there something somebody hasn't told me?

In the blue corner, CHRISTOPHER MATTHEW

'Derrick,' I told the chairman of the Headington Branch of the Oxford Conservative Association, 'don't think I don't appreciate the opportunity you're offering me. I realise that this is the big one . . .'

'Look,' he said, 'all you have to do is knock at the door and when it opens, say, "Good evening. John Patten, the Conservative candidate, is in the neighbourhood. Would you like to speak to him"?'

I pointed out that, even so, I couldn't see how a sharp fist on the nose from a sixteen-stone Cowley assembly plant foreman was going to further the cause of the Conservative party one iota, and that the right arm I was being asked to give in order to ensure Mrs T.'s serene passage to No 10 was made for better things than pressing doorbells and raising door-knockers.

On the other hand, it's given to few of us in these days of electronic electioneering to experience a General Election at grass roots level, to test the nation's pulse for oneself, and dip one's toe in the water of public opinion. Confrontation with the man in the street would be nothing if not instructive . . .

We met after tea outside the Black Boy public house. There was Sholto, a budding lawyer; Bob, a jolly butcher; Vic, fair-haired and reassuringly bulky in his business suit; and Nigel, a poet and painter, to whom I, as a novice knocker-up, was assigned. He wore his responsibilities remarkably lightly, I thought. But then I suppose if you live locally, political acumen plays very much second fiddle to cheerful familiarity.

The fact that our candidate was five minutes late was not reassuring. However, when the official Austin Princess drew up, plastered with blue stickers and chauffeured by the President of the Oxford University Conservative Association, all fears melted away in the pale evening sunshine.

Thirty-three years old and a Fellow of Hertford College, John Patten strode towards us, dark hair bouncing confidently, blue rosette twinkling in his lapel, an eager smile playing across his youthful features, right hand already thrust forward in greeting. Suddenly one was aware of a feeling of heightened anticipation, rather like the time Richard Todd came into a restaurant where I was eating and sat at the next table. The scent of the chase was in our nostrils; the game was afoot; the 1979 General Election had, for me, come alive at last.

We fanned out into Barton Lane. The others bustled on ahead and disappeared up various drives. Nigel and I took the house opposite. I left the talking to my more experienced colleague.

'Good evening. John Patten, the Conservative candidate is here . . .'

'Oh, rather,' said the man enthusiastically, and we hurried on past our colleagues who were standing on doorsteps, smiling a good deal and engaging the owners in electioneering small talk while awaiting the arrival of the great man himself.

By the time we turned up Chestnut Avenue, we had left our candidate far behind.

'He's doing a lot of talking this evening,' muttered Derrick striding past.

So, as a result, were we.

'I'm not sure if we're registered,' said the man in the corner house – a don at Magdalen.

We were not to be put off that easily.

'Well,' I said coaxingly, 'why not talk to him anyway?'

'I'd be happy to talk to *him*' said the don, 'but not to you.'

'Rather uncalled for, I thought,' said Nigel as we headed on up the avenue.

By now we were in semi-detached country, where elections are won or lost. Now we could expect a few fireworks.

'Oh dear,' muttered our first conquest, a middle-aged lady in apron and slippers. 'I don't suppose he'd want to meet *us*.'

I daresay she was right, but he did anyway.

'Hullo, dear,' he cried, bounding down the path, hand out-stretched. 'How are *you*?'

There was a notice on her door announcing NO JOBS. Whether this was a political slogan, a cry for help, or a discouragement to Boy Scouts, I did not manage to discover, and never shall. So much to do, so little time.

In Hawthorn Avenue we were brusquely informed by a husky young man in jeans and a vest that meeting John Patten was a pleasure he could happily forego. I thought for a moment we might be in for some political hurly-burly, but to my astonishment my senior colleague merely smiled politely and walked away. I'd have thought he'd have seized this opportunity to convert the heathen, but perhaps in Conservative circles that might be considered impolite.

In Ash Grove, I met my first ever BL striker. He was immensely cheerful and solidly pro-Thatcher. No hope of confrontation there. The cut and thrust of political debate was evidently not for us that evening.

The caravanserai turned into Blackthorn Close about halfway through *This Is Your Life*. By crouching slightly, I could just glimpse it through the Venetian blinds of our first target. By a coincidence, the subject was Ian Ogilvy, always a particular favourite of mine, and I happened to know a couple of the people taking part.

After a long while a woman opened the door and informed us that, given a choice between John Patten and *The Saint*, she knew which she'd choose.

I laughed and said that, oddly enough, I'd rather been looking forward to that particular programme.

'Oh yes?' she said.

'We were just watching it through your window.'

'We saw you,' she said. 'Gave us quite a turn.'

'Actually, we know some people who are in it,' said Nigel.

'I wouldn't mind betting Ian Ogilvy votes Conservative,' I added, peering through the open door at the television set.

'That's as may be,' said the woman, 'but I'm still not going to invite you in.' And she closed the door in our faces.

I think we can count on her vote on the 3rd.

We called it a day soon after that. John Patten went off with his wife, Louise, and Douglas Hurd to a public meeting in Cheney School, and I went off on my own to London, secure in the knowledge that in this great country of ours, this throne of kings, this sceptred isle, each and every one of us has a small, but I believe not insignificant part to play in the shaping of our destiny.

Graham's Election Night

'Where the hell is Billericay, anyway?'

'If I don't drink it to celebrate victory, it'll comfort me in defeat.'

'Just a minute, Phyllis – how **did** you vote?'

'It's a much more interesting election than 1970,
when we didn't have colour.'

'You could take advantage of this lull to empty your
ashtray again'.

'I don't know how Alastair Burnet feels after all that,
but I'm whacked.'

Punch, 27 February 1974

JOHN McWILLIAM MP

I arrived during an election to visit a Salvation Army band practice. As I walked in they struck up with 'Here comes the conquering hero' in a musical show of political loyalties.

'Thank you', I said. 'What did you play when the Tory candidate came?'

'Oh, we gave him "Rescue the perish-ed," ' said the captain.

I presume that on election day they played 'Show me the way to go home' because I lost.

MICHAEL BLACKMAN (activist)

Three years ago, during a Hertfordshire County Council election, I called on a would-be voter asking for his support. The surprising reply was: 'I'll vote for you if you restore capital punishment.' I explained politely that Tring Liberals did not have the power to do this but hinted that if there were a sufficient groundswell in nearby Aldbury, we could perhaps restore the ancient stocks for a flogging festival.

DENIS HOWELL MP

When canvassing for a 'Yes' vote in the Common Market referendum, a voter responded by saying that he would definitely vote in favour of remaining in Europe since Israel was a member. I replied in all honesty that, though delighted by this pledge of support, I had to make it clear that Israel was not a member of the European Economic Community. The voter replied: 'Oh yes, they must be. They're always in the Eurovision Song Contest.'

ROBIN CORBETT MP

It was the 1974 'Who Rules Britain?' election with the miners strike, power cuts and the three-day week. 'Are you going to vote Labour?' I asked the lady at the door. 'I'm not voting for anyone,' she replied firmly. 'Not until I have black plastic rubbish bags like they do two streets up.'

'So if I get you some plastic bags . . . ?'

'Yes,' she answered, 'you'll have my vote.'

She had them within the hour. My majority, including her, was 485!

GWYNETH DUNWOODY MP

During the second 1974 election when the Leader of my party, Harold Wilson, would soon be Prime Minister again, I was stopped in the middle of Crewe by a man who told me rather fiercely: 'I'm voting for you because I can't stand that Harold Wilson.' I never said a word. Just smiled and left.

2
Nudes Behind the Knockers

VIC TURTON (former Lord Mayor of Birmingham)

I knocked on a door and a lady's voice said, 'Just a minute.' When the door opened, I saw her standing there . . . in her underclothes. We stared at each other for several seconds, myself in amazement and herself in some other frame of mind. Finally, glancing discreetly up the road, she nodded, and said: 'My husband's on nights, come in.'

DENIS HOWELL MP

I came to one of the doors in Unett Street, which had those back-to-back houses where you walked straight from the street into the living room, and gave a loud knock. I heard a lady's voice say 'Come in, dear.' Naturally, I opened the door and was extremely embarrassed to find the lady of the house without a stitch on and standing in front of the fireplace. Seeing my discomfiture, I am glad to say that she immediately tried to put me at my ease. 'Oh, I am sorry,' she said 'I thought you were the man from the Co-op.'

MALCOLM HAYWARD (agent)

During the Stafford by-election on a warm, sultry morning and armed with canvass card and posters, I set off in search of the Conservative vote.

After about half-an-hour and using my 'Sorry you were out' cards at a rapid rate, I knocked on a front door which was answered by a four-year-old little girl.

'Is Mummy in?' I asked.

'Mummy's round the back,' she answered.

'Could you fetch Mummy?'

'Mummy's round the back.'

So I followed her round the back . . . to where Mummy was sunbathing in the nude. No, I didn't run. I stuck to the job in hand and asked her – looking carefully at her eyes – whether the Conservatives could count on her support. I received a sharp 'No!' though it was obvious from her colour – bright red – that she was a Labour supporter.

I was three doors up from the sunbathing lady when I posted another 'Sorry you were out' card, turned to go out the gate and came face-to-face with a snarling Alsatian. The fences separating the houses were quite small so I decided to run and jump the fence into the next garden and make my exit that way.

The dog did not follow so I jumped the next fence and the next . . . and found myself back with the naked lady again!

JOHN WARDEN (Political Editor, *Daily Express*)

An MP in the Midlands was greeted with a friendly, 'Come in!' before he had even said a word. Inside the discreetly lit hallway he introduced himself: 'I am your Conservative candidate.'

Gales of laughter: 'We're all for free enterprise here, aren't we girls?'

Anyway, they took a poster and put it in the window and he never knew whether it did more for their trade than his.

RAY GREEN (activist)

A pair of us were canvassing a block of flats in the Midlands. We knocked on the door of Flat 3 and it swung open but nobody appeared. After a few nervous seconds, we cleared our throats, knocked again – and then my friend looked around the door. There, between the door and the wall, stood a woman. Completely naked. My friend did not pause for breath. 'Can we count on your support?' he asked. She said we definitely could. Then we closed the door and made for the lift, in fits of laughter. As the lift doors opened, a man rushed out and asked the way to Flat No. 3. We got into the lift and I pointed the way while my friend said: 'Hurry up, mate. She's waiting for you.' Then the lift doors closed . . .

JOHN McWILLIAM MP

After the canvasser had knocked, the door was opened by a young lady freshly out of the bath and wrapped in a bath towel tucked in at one side.

'Sorry to bother you,' he said, 'but will you be voting Labour?'

'Labour?' she spat. 'You'll be lucky!' The words were hardly out when the towel dropped from her glistening body.

RICHARD SIMMONDS MEP

During the first campaign for the European Elections in 1979, I was accompanied by the then Westminster candidate on a canvassing expedition into what afterwards turned out to be the red light district of Wolverhampton.

Our joint door-knocking and the subsequent question 'Can I count on your support?' elicited some fairly unorthodox replies, ranging from 'One at a time, dearie', to 'You can count on anything of mine, provided it's paid for.'

PAT JOLLY (former Labour agent)

The social security claimant was told she couldn't have her money because she was co-habiting. As the parliamentary candidate couldn't get to see her, I was deputed to help and I was conscious of my responsibilities.

I knocked on the door but there was no reply, though I did notice the light was on, music playing and after another loud knock, the curtains twitched. Finally, after another bout of knocking, the door opened and a weedy-looking man dressed only in a shirt, opened it a crack.

'Is Mrs Smith in?' I asked. The door opened wider and I came inside a one-bedroomed flat – really a cupboard with a toilet. Mrs Smith was indeed in – she was in the bed, her naked shoulders peeping out of the sheet. The man in the shirt then climbed back into the bed and I was put to the trouble of explaining why we might not be able to help with the social security.

A Matter of Opinion

J. W. TAYLOR'S clip-board among the pollsters

*'Certainly I'll give you my opinion,
young man.'*

'There's a swing to political apathy.'

'And now wilt **thou** answer **me** a few
simple questions?'

'Well now, to get back to my original reason
for accosting you . . .'

'Don't know.'   Punch, 9 October 1974

3
An Eccentric Guide to Politics

JAMES CASLAKE (activist)

Canvassing an elderly gentleman who said he didn't want to hear anything that the SDP had to say, I suggested he ought to hear all sides of the story before he made up his mind.

The gentleman asked, rather angrily, why anyone needed to hear both sides of any story and when I told him that was what democracy was all about, shouted, 'I'm not interested in democracy; I'm in the Labour Party.'

BILL BOOTH (activist)

Canvassing in a Ewell village, the lady of the house told me: 'We're not interested in politics. We're Conservatives.'

ROGER KING MP

A nervous young man came into my advice bureau.

'I'm being spied on by MI5,' he said.

'Oh yes,' I asked. 'How do you know?'

'Because they follow me around and shine lights on my bedroom window.'

'What do your parents think?'

'They think I'm mad,' he responded.

I decided to humour him.

'Did "they" follow you here?'

'Yes. A car in front and a car behind,' he answered.

'Oh?' I said quickly. 'How did the lead car know where you were going?'

'Ah, my phone's being tapped as well.'

ROBERT RHODES JAMES MP

One of my favourites was at my first by-election nine years ago, when a lady rushed at me waving my election literature screaming: 'I will never vote for you.' When I enquired why, she replied, 'Because you were born in India.' I explained patiently that my father was in the Indian Army and my mother happened to be with him at the time. 'I do not care,' she replied 'you're foreign. I am voting National Front.'

J. S. SCRUTON (activist)

One evening during a Council election, I was canvassing in North Hill. An elderly and charming lady listened politely to what I had to say about our Liberal candidate, pondered a moment, and then replied most gravely and courteously that she always voted Conservative because she didn't believe in party politics.

Messing About in Votes

(Punch, 25 May 1983)

JONATHAN SALE

'The El Toffo Upper Class Twit was disqualified for issuing a smear leaflet.'

This is not, as it happens, the dirtiest election during recorded history (although the outpourings of Paul 'Eatanswill' Johnson in the *Daily Mail* give it some claim to that title). We have to go back to 1962 for that.

There was not, as psephologists will immediately point out, a general election in that year but there was something of far greater import: the great Cambridge Union Presidential Election Scandal. There was one of those every term – presidential elections, that is – but none of such ferocity, involving as it did, at the end of the summer, a contest between a Communist and an American who, if not actually funded by the CIA, was believed to have a divine mission to bring a breath of the Cold War wherever he trod.

Where he trod on election day was into a room equipped with a bar and packed with students. In offering drinks all round to any floating voters prepared to drift his way (as the prosecution alleged) he infringed the regulations on election expenses; there weren't supposed to be any, and all canvassing was forbidden.

When the returns were counted, he won by a whisker, only to be challenged by his opponent over the matter of the drinks bill. There was an official – insofar as anything organised by students can be official – enquiry, which resulted in the American ending up on a plane headed for the States and a CIA debriefing, while the Communist went off in a huff, to console himself with either his copy of *Das Kapital* or his Economics Finals.

The second was the more likely study, because if he achieved a First, he would be able to stay on for a fourth year, which would permit him to stand again for the Union. It was at this point that the saga took on all the elements of a schoolboy's yarn – 'The Fifth Form at St Trotsky's' – perhaps.

Brian Pollitt, as our hero, the son of the legendary Thirties Lefty Harry Pollitt, was called, was asleep in his room early one morning when person or persons still unknown burst in and beat him up, badly. Nothing unusual in that, you might say, just the Far Right indulging in its standard method of political dialogue. What made it more extraordinary was that particular attention was devoted to damaging his writing hand. Unable to perform in the examination room, he would clearly be prevented from getting a First and staying on to head the Union.

That was not how the story ended. Dictating his answers from his sick bed, Pollitt made the national news bulletins by still achieving a First. By the time I went up to Cambridge in the autumn, he was safely ensconced in the Presidential chair, swept there by a massive vote of sympathy. He was, incidentally, a very good President.

The lesson to be drawn from all this is, apart from the advisability of locking the bedroom door, that passions as great as those of a General Election can be aroused when two people are competing for the same post, however minor it may be. That is why people got rid of their monarchs; once a king is in power; there can be no reselection committees, ten per cent swings, Don't Knows and victory celebrations, until someone invents democracy.

Democracy is thriving at the nearest student body to the *Punch* offices, that of the LSE. The Don't Knows won in the election that brought the current General Secretary, Tony Donaldson, to power; only thirty-five per cent voted.

'It was not a clean campaign,' he alleged. 'I was compared to Ken Livingstone.' It could have been worse: 'That wasn't intended to be a compliment but I took it as one.' It could have been a lot worse. Being compared to the GLC leader is better than a slap round the belly with a wet fish and much better than a British Fascist playing football with your right hand.

Personalities were involved in the campaign but not the Cold War; issues ranged from course contents to the coffee bar, although some of the thirteen standing, such as the Nomadic Afghan Tribes Candidate, may well have been fighting on slightly different battlegrounds. The last contestant was one of the jokers in the electoral pack, unlike the Democratic Student Front Candidate, who was believed to be for real and was thought to be a front organisation for the Revolutionary Communist Party of Great Britain (Marxist Leninist). This is not the same Revolutionary Communist Party as stood in Bermondsey the other month (although the votes acquired, well into double figures, were much the same) but another one, which holds that Albania is the sole nation on the world's surface to follow the right political tack.

There is little for the pundits to extrapolate from the LSE results. If the swing recorded there was reproduced on a national basis, Labour (Donaldson) would romp home, followed by the Alliance (down from its previous Number One), then an Independent, with the Conservative in a deposit-losing fourth. Make what you will of the fact that a Surrealist polled seventy votes (as against Labour's 450). The El Toffo Upper-Class Twit was disqualified for issuing a smear leaflet. Be warned, Paul Johnson.

'From time to time there are joke candidates and sometimes they are elected,' admitted Mrs Mary Marsh, Deputy Head of St Christopher School, Letchworth. Still, she can't complain; the same is true of the Mother of Parliaments. St Christopher makes the House of Commons look like the Court of Richard III; the Head Boy and Head Girl are elected by the Senior School, as are Games Secretaries, Chairman of the Library Committee and the discussion body known as the School Council.

Re-selection isn't in it. The Head Boys and Girl are out on their ears at the end of their (single term) of office, while 'Elected Councillors who fail to attend two consecutive Council meetings shall be subject to re-election.' Proportional Representation is used: 'The voting papers shall be divided into piles according to the first name on their lists. Each paper on the smallest pile shall then be transferred according to the next name . . .' and so on.

'We spend quite a lot of time on elections,' agreed Mrs Marsh, but she reassured me that no campaigning is allowed, save for the issuing of a brief biography with details such as which teams the candidate had played for.

All this sounds as refreshing as Franco's death must have seemed to the Spanish Republicans, particularly if like me, you remembered the way in which the Headmaster's Junta would make the decision as to which of the quislings among their pupils was worthy of high office. St Christopher even runs to a Visitors' Gallery: 'Anybody not a member of Council who wishes to attend a Council Meeting should obtain permission and should sit in the back two rows.' The only missing element is a Press Gallery in which the lads and lasses from the school magazine can sit and pen satirical remarks about their betters.

It is a long way from the arcane system used until recently by the Conservative Party to elect its leader. This resembled the old-fashioned appointment of prefects in a backward public school; the Party would wait expectantly and suddenly someone like Alec Douglas-Home would turn out to be wearing the crown. (Nowadays a more democratic process gives them someone like Margaret Thatcher, which just shows that all progress is not necessarily progressive.) 'A Magic Circle,' was how Harold Wilson described it, to arouse immediate anger from the band of magicians who use that name for themselves.

Last week I talked to Geoffrey Robinson, Treasurer of the Magic Circle to check on its democratic principles. The idea of counting votes cast by light-fingered gents who can produce rabbits out of hats and flags from thin air, does not appeal and it may be just as well that official places fall vacant rather more frequently than magical operatives can be found to fill them.

'The last contest I can remember was for my own job, when my predecessor and I both put up for Treasurer. He won but then he went and died' – foul play not suspected, police are *not* looking for a black-caped man with a wand and a machine for sawing ladies in half – 'and I stepped in.'

He has been there ever since and, given his abilities, would be a hard man to budge. Questioned about his professional skills, he explained: 'I cut up a piece of rope twice and tie the ends together – and it becomes one whole piece again. For my next trick, I borrow a pound note from a member of the audience and burn it. Then I hand him a box, which he unlocks, to find another box, which he unlocks to find an egg. He breaks the egg; inside is a walnut. He is asked to stamp on it; there is the pound note, which is handed back to its owner.'

As an electoral platform, it-beats making a three-minute speech about the Common Market. Mr Robinson is fine, so long as he looks after his right hand, and, possibly, right sleeve. Of course, I've only his word for all that. You know what sort of promises people make when they're standing for office.

LIEUT. COLONEL LESLIE HUXTABLE (activist)

Some years ago while giving mutual aid in an East End constituency, my knock on the door was answered by a very Cockney gentleman. On hearing who I was, he shouted over his shoulder for 'Mary'. Thinking he was shouting for his wife, I warmed to the prospect and continued with my spiel. After some minutes, he repeated his shout for 'Mary' who still had not appeared and I continued talking. Again he repeated the name, rather more irritably and 'Mary', a fully grown Alsatian dog with fangs gleaming, headed straight down the passage at me. I covered the five or six yards to the garden gate in two seconds flat so I have no idea whether she had a little lamb or not.

NEIL KINNOCK MP

One jaded June evening in the sun-soaked election of 1970 I summoned up final reserves of bonhomie and bounced down a garden path extending a warm smile, the hand of friendship and a cheery introduction – only to be met with an Anglo-Saxon instruction to go away.

For the first time in twelve years of electioneering, civility evaporated. I offered a brief address to the citizen on his parentage and intelligence, throwing in a few unhelpful and physically unattainable suggestions about the future storage of his gardening implements.

Minutes later, I was greeted by his neighbours delightedly informing me that my chastisement of the Scourge of the Street had won their votes.

SIR JOHN OSBORN MP

It so happened that I had a constituent who had been a regular complainant before she emigrated to British Colombia with her husband, and whilst I was on my way to Canada on Commonwealth Parliamentary business she wrote, again, beefing about the injustice being perpetrated by Prime Minister Trudeau.

My secretary forwarded this letter to the hotel I was staying at in Vancouver, and I opened it on arrival. Seeing my constituent's telephone number, I rang her immediately. 'This is John Osborn, your Member of Parliament from the Hallam Constituency of

Sheffield. I have got your letter about the repatriation of the Canada Act.' 'Oh, Mr Osborn, how kind of you to ring, particularly all the way to Vancouver.' I explained I was not telephoning from Sheffield; that I had actually arrived in Vancouver. There was a pause, and my constituent said, 'Oh dear . . . oh dear me. I know how conscientious you have been Mr Osborn, but what about the expenses!? You should have asked me first, you see – I never intended you to come out here.' 'We'll worry about the expense question later; the fact is that I am here, I am going to visit the provincial government in Victoria tomorrow, and if you want to know the outcome please ring me back at my hotel and I will be only too happy to discuss the matter with you.'

I have not heard from that particular constituent, now ex-constituent, since that phone call.

BILL BOOTH (Liberal activist)

Arriving at a house to give the lady a lift to the polling station, I found another Liberal car as well. The lady was extremely apologetic, saying her daughter, unbeknown to her, had also phoned our headquarters for a car. 'Don't give it a second thought', I said. 'Oh, but you must have something for your trouble,' she mumbled, fishing behind the door for a shopping bag out of which she produced . . . two toilet rolls.

ROBIN CORBETT MP

Last-day canvassing before the General Election took me past a house which was adorned with several Liberal posters. I was just walking past, when the occupant darted out. 'You can count on my vote tomorrow,' he said.

'But what about those posters?'

'Oh, take no notice of those,' said the man. 'I don't like to let people know how I vote.'

TREVOR LINDLEY (activist)

Keith Kyle was a Labour candidate in the late '60s and the BBC did a series of films on his campaign. The final film concerned Election Day, and the final sequence was of Keith knocking on a door. A voice came from inside: 'Hello?' Cameras whirred. Keith called blithely: 'It's Keith Kyle, your Labour candidate. Have you been to vote yet?' A long silence. 'No, I'll go tomorrow.'

PETER ARCHER MP

Many years ago, before the word 'feminism' was coined, I knocked on a door which was opened by a middle-aged lady. I explained my mission, whereupon she turned and bellowed upstairs: ' 'Arry, they've come about the voting.' There was an inaudible reply. ' 'Ow are ya goin' ta vote?' There was a further inaudible reply. 'Yer votin' Tory? OK, Tory'.

She turned to me: 'You 'eard that.' Then she lowered her voice to a whisper and added, 'Then I'm votin' Labour. I'd do anythin' ter spite him'.

FRED TUCKMAN MEP

Canvassing in Nottingham during the 1979 elections, I had to explain to the posh lady in the detached house at the end of a long drive, that I was standing as a Tory for the *European* elections. 'Europe', she said, 'but that's abroad!'

'I'd prefer not to discuss the Euro-election. I haven't been too well lately and the doctor says I mustn't get over-excited.'

Reproduced by kind permission of the *Guardian*

ROSEMARY POCKLEY (activist)

I was canvassing in Stubbington for myself, in the local borough elections. As I walked around one estate, I noticed that one of my posters had been stuck in a window, but that it had fallen down so though the photograph was visible, the name was not. I knocked on the door which was answered by a man in pyjamas and dressing gown.

'Good afternoon,' I said, 'Thank you very much for displaying my poster in your window. However, I wonder if you realized that it had fallen down?'

He beamed at me. 'Oh yes I know, I put it like that myself. I knew you would be bound to notice and I wanted to make sure you would call on me, so that we could have a nice chat. Do come in, my dear. I have been waiting for you all day.'

I ran, and it wasn't for the Conservative Party.

WILLIAM WILSON (County Councillor)

After I had been returned as the Member for Coventry South I walked the streets thanking my electorate, and I was going back to my car when I saw two boys, each about five years old. One said to me, 'Are you Wilson?' I replied that I was. 'My mam voted for you,' said the boy. The other, a more diffident lad, shuffled his feet. 'And what about you, young man?' I ventured. 'My mam did not vote. She said neither of the buggers was worth voting for.'

4
Beware of the Pets

SIR GEORGE YOUNG MP

This is a true story! A Tory canvasser crunched his way up the gravel drive to a large, detached house. About to ring the bell, his ankles were snapped at by a yapping, small dog. He rang. An upstairs window opened and a woman leaned out. She listened to his request for support and replied: 'Yes, that's okay. We're always Tory.'

'Thank you,' said the canvasser as the dog mounted another attack. 'Kick his balls,' the woman advised.

'We don't do that sort of thing in the Conservative Party,' said the canvasser. The woman laughed. 'No, it's all right. Just kick his balls.'

The canvasser screwed up his courage and delivered the toe of his shoe to the dog's tender parts.

As he pulled his leg back, he saw two tennis balls lying on the ground.

DAVID MUDD MP

It was one of *those* roads, anonymous, repetitive. Obvious signs warned me of a high canine density . . . letter-boxes set low in front doors were clearly designed to entice unwary leaflet-bearing fingers into a snarling and toothy greeting.

Number 49 was different. The letter box was set high. Showing encouragement to my canvassers, I volunteered to do *that* one. My fingers slipped through the box . . . and I needed three stitches as my finger was slashed by a high-flying cat!

JIM LESTOR MP (Cons)

While out canvassing in the 1983 election, I encountered a pet shop with a number of unusual pets including a tarantula and a skunk. The pet shop owner, a Tory supporter, introduced the skunk as 'Denis Healey'. This was a joke apparently not appreciated by the skunk who promptly bit the pet shop owner. Fortunately, he had chosen to leave the tarantula nameless.

KENNETH WARREN MP

During the General Election I was speeding my canvassing by running from house to house. Rushing up one pathway to meet a lady of mature years, I thrust out my hand in greeting and before I could say 'I hope you will vote for me', I thought my hand had been bitten by a dog. I looked down and to my horror saw she was holding her dentures!

SIMON BURNS (activist)

During a Bank Holiday in the 1983 election campaign I drove up a long drive which had a fire smoking out of the chimney. I knocked on the door and someone called out 'Hello'. I waited but no one came. So I knocked again. 'Hello,' came the reply and I waited and listened but could not hear anyone coming. The whole sequence happened again and as no one came to the door, I called out who I was and what I was doing there. When I finished speaking, I heard another 'Hello' and, through the porch window, saw I had been conversing with a Mynah bird.

MRS V. PURSER (activist)

An elderly man out canvassing was about to enter my sister's front gate when her golden retriever dashed down the path barking furiously. The dog jumped up and put her paws firmly on top of the gate, seemingly barring entry. Looking somewhat alarmed, the man decided not to attempt to open the gate. Showing great presence of mind, he popped an election leaflet into the surprised dog's open mouth and moved up the road, leaving her to pad back up the path, proudly carrying her prize.

BOP PARSONS (activist)

I once lost a vote for the candidate by taking my dog canvassing with me – he bit a potential voter's cat at the door.

SIR JOHN BIGGS-DAVISON MP

During my canvassing, I opened a gate at the bottom of a large garden leading up to a little house and a fierce Alsatian about the size of a donkey galloped down the path towards me, showing a full set of teeth. The door of the house was flung open by the lady owner, who would surely bring the brute to heel. 'Call him Rover!' she yelled helpfully. 'He *probably* won't bite you!'

JIM LESTOR MP (Cons)

When I called with my chairman at one house, an enormous dog bounded over the restraining fence and tore the literature out of the hand of my chairman. A lady subsequently appeared at the door and, seeing our blue rosettes, commented, 'Good dog! Good boy!'

ROBERT KILROY-SILK MP

This story is attributed to the late Simon Mahon, MP for Bootle.

The canvasser headed up the path towards a front door and saw a large dog lying on the lawn. As he walked to the door, the dog joined him.

The couple inside were frantic with worry as their 18-year-old daughter had disappeared and invited the canvasser in. As he tried to reassure them, tea and sandwiches were served. When no-one was looking, the dog snatched two sandwiches off the low table. 'Badly trained dog,' thought the canvasser. A little later it cocked its leg against an armchair. 'I'd stop that kind of thing,' he mused.

Leaving with pledges of help when his candidate was elected, the canvasser headed up the path. The front door re-opened and a voice called. 'Excuse me, you've forgotten your dog.'

ROBIN CORBETT MP

A canvasser was told that the voter would not support any candidate unless he or she was an animal lover. 'Oh, Robin's very keen on animal welfare, I'll call him,' said the canvasser.

I got to the open door, shook the voter's hand and a black cat sped past me, down the path and into the road. A squeal of brakes followed as the poor cat was run down and killed.

SIR WILLIAM CLARK MP

My wife and I were canvassing during a General Election in Northampton where I was the Conservative Parliamentary candidate. My wife called at one door and the lady, after being told the purpose of the visit, said, 'I am delighted to see you, do come in.' My wife tried to avoid entering but the lady was insistent and said, 'I want you to meet a friend of mine. If he likes you, I'll vote for your husband.' We were duly ushered in and presented to the lady's budgerigar.

NICHOLAS LYELL MP

Canvassing one morning in a small town in my constituency, I saw a young woman weeding her garden beneath a rose trellis. I walked across and introduced myself as her Conservative candidate. 'No, you are not,' she said, giving me a stony stare. I protested mildly that even if she did not support us, I was her candidate and I asked whom she did support. 'No-one,' she replied equally coldly. 'If there were a Marxist, I might support him.' At this moment, she got up and moved a few steps down the garden as though keeping an eye open for a small child. 'Have you got children?' I asked, seeking, without much hope, to be friendly. 'No,' she replied, 'a snake.'

I looked up and there, on the rose trellis, was indeed an enormous snake. 'How interesting,' I said faintly, retreating a pace or two. 'What kind is it?'

'A python', she replied. Well, that was good news. At least this snake was not poisonous, contenting itself with merely swallowing its victims whole!

DAVID MARTIN MEP

In the middle of a Sunday afternoon canvass of a street of Edinburgh tenements full of empty flats and people who had no interest in European elections, the canvasser found all the residents out on the stairs.

One occupier was away for the weekend and a neighbour had undertaken to feed the dog which was now at bay on the landing, barking furiously.

My intrepid supporter, having seen that the massive noise level was coming from a spaniel, walked up the stairs and sat down next to it.

Far from chewing off his rosette or his hand, the frightened beast slowly calmed down and started licking both. He may have won over a few votes for Socialism.

CROSSBENCHER (*Sunday Express*)

Mrs Thatcher has obviously upset the dogs of Britain. When Mr Peter Rost MP was out canvassing he had a chunk taken out of his corduroy jeans and leg by a large hound. Since the owner, if not the dog, was a Tory, he offered to pay for the damage but Mr Rost gallantly refused.

Somewhat less gallant was a Labour candidate. When his opponent was similarly set upon by an aggressive dog, the Labour man sent a 'Get Well Soon' card. To the dog.

ROBIN CORBETT MP

It was a lovely evening for canvassing and my aide and I were having a good conversation on the doorstep with a voter who was definitely swinging in our direction. Suddenly, my aide grabbed my hand and said: 'Fine, but we're late for an appointment and must rush . . . thank you and I hope we can count on your support' . . . and he dashed off with me in hot pursuit. 'That was daft,' I told him, 'another couple of minutes and we could have swung his vote.'

'Forget his vote, you won't get it,' said my aide, a most experienced canvasser. 'I could see what you couldn't. We'd interrupted his supper and while he was talking to us, I saw his dog get on the chair and wolf the whole lot up.'

DAVID MITCHELL MP

While electioneering near Andover in the last election, the door was opened by an attractive young woman. While explaining who I was and asking for her support, we were joined by a beautiful red setter. I leaned forward, patted the dog and continued: 'Aren't you lovely, aren't you beautiful? I would like to take you home with me.' There then occurréd a minor explosion from behind a curtain and the husband of the house emerged to ascertain who I was addressing: the dog or his wife.

Put down that nice young man, Tiddles!

5
Canvassing and Other Catastrophes

DENIS HOWELL MP

I was canvassing my constituency in Birmingham. 'Hello, Mrs Papadopulous,' I said to one voter. 'Can I count on your support as usual?'

'No, you can't,' said Mrs Papadopulous. 'I'm not voting for you because of your party's immigration policy.'

'But, Mrs Papadopulous, if it wasn't for our immigration policy, *Mr* Papadopulous wouldn't have been allowed into the country.'

'And that's *exactly* why I'm not voting for you,' said my ex-voter.

KEN LIVINGSTONE

In 1984 the Labour Group on the GLC precipitated four by-elections in protest at the Government's abolition plans. However, London Tories – under instructions from Mrs Thatcher – decided not to field candidates, and a virtual newspaper blackout followed, in an attempt to minimize the effect of our gesture. I was one of the candidates, in the Paddington seat. After about a week of campaigning, with virtually no press coverage at all, my press officer Nita Clarke, in desperation, phoned TVAM to see if there was any way they would get me on the programme, which had often invited me on when I was still GLC leader.

After some discussion, the programme organizers agreed, but only if I would do something I had been resisting for months –

appear with Lizzie, their early morning exercise expert, doing aerobic exercises to disco music, dressed in sports gear.

I resisted for a while, but was finally persuaded. I appeared on air at around eight o'clock in the morning, feeling the biggest idiot it is possible to imagine. TVAM provided me with a grey track suit, because I put my foot down about the crimson shorts and T-shirt originally suggested.

The exercises were murder. Anyone who knows me will confirm just how unco-ordinated I am and exercising to music just made it worse. After a minute I ached all over, and Lizzie's cries of 'stretch that muscle' and 'come on Ken, it's supposed to hurt' added insult to injury. Five minutes later, I had finished. The interviewer concluded the proceedings with a reference to my face, now the colour of beetroot as a result of my exertions. 'Well,' he said blithely, from the comfort of his chair, 'that face certainly gives a whole new meaning to the name Red Ken.'

Despite my embarrassment, the stunt certainly worked. Throughout the rest of the campaign on the streets of Paddington, voters would accost me with 'I saw you on the telly, doing your exercises. You looked a proper charley,' or words to that effect.

There's a footnote to the story. My Liberal opponent demanded equal time from TVAM, to do his exercises, too. They turned him down – and frankly I think he was lucky. It's hard to maintain your dignity as a serious politician while flinging your arms and legs about in different directions and trying to touch your toes for the first time in ten years.

Incidentally, I won the by-election with an increased majority.

HUMFREY MALINS MP

To attract the Chinese vote, my neighbouring candidate in Scotland Exchange asked a Chinese friend to prepare large posters with the words 'Please cast your vote for X' written in Chinese. We delivered and put up over 400 posters in the Chinese quarter. A few days later we began to notice a distinct chill in the atmosphere. It turned out that our friend had transcribed on to the posters, in Chinese, the phrase: 'Get Knotted Says X.'

ANTHONY SIMPSON MEP

During the 1984 Euro Election campaign I was campaigning in a country district, Northamptonshire being a *very rural* county, when we saw a potential voter clipping a hedge along the roadside. Not wishing to lose the opportunity to introduce myself, we stopped and I leapt out of the car, introduced myself to our topiarist and urged him to support me. Following a non-committal reply, I leapt smartly back into the car only to hear, and feel, a ripping across the seat of my trousers. They had indeed split. That will teach me to buy my suits in Taiwan!

For the rest of the day electors in Northamptonshire may have wondered why, with the temperatures in the high 80s, the Conservative candidate was campaigning in a raincoat!

CLLR FRED ROSE (Birmingham)

'No, I can't vote,' said the middle-aged woman, 'I've not got my teeth in – can't find them.'

Canvasser: 'If that's all the trouble, have mine,' he said, removing his own dentures with a flourish.

JOHN WATSON MP

When I was fighting York (and York was fighting back with some alacrity) there was really only one street where the houses were so visibly affluent that I could rely upon Conservative support without even canvassing.

To cheer myself up after a particularly depressing week (it was the October 1974 election), I decided to canvass that particular road.

I strode up one impressive gravel drive, knocked on the door, and was surprised to have it answered by a butler. As one might expect, I was invited in for pre-dinner drinks and, five sherries later, walked back down the gravel drive feeling that the election might not be lost after all.

I walked seventy yards along the road and up the next drive. When I banged on the door it was the same house – just a different entrance. The house owner (and the butler) told me that since our last conversation they had just seen a Conservative party broadcast on television and would now be voting Labour.

Party Lines

(Punch, 9 October 1974)

According to the latest Punch poll, 52.3% of the electorate said they were going to an Election Night party, 2% said they weren't, and

25.8% said they were not prepared to commit themselves at this moment in time. Clearly, political jargon and posturing, not to mention the continuous tellyblast of the night itself, is going to have its effect on the partygoers, too . . .

'I say, I'm awfully sorry, Dennis, but Maureen has just been sick on that rather nice Kazakh rug of yours.'

'Ah, yes, well, I can't say that the result was altogether unexpected, Arthur. Maureen is one of those rather curious examples that can go either way. I remember in 1971 she put away two bottles of Vat 69 and still managed to get through eighty-six verses of *Eskimo Nell* without fluffing once. What do you think, Norman?'

'I agree with you, Dennis, although it has to be said that Maureen is something of a freak example this year. Remember, there have been basic changes in her shape since 1971. And you have to bear in mind that she *has* been on vodka this time, which has thrown out all our calculations somewhat!'

'What do you think this will mean for the evening as a whole, Jeffrey?'

'Well, it's terribly hard to predict at this stage, Dennis, she *is* one of the first results we've seen, but if the rest of the guests go the way Maureen has gone, I think we may well see you redecorating in the coming weeks . . .'

'. . . must say you're looking absolutely gorgeous tonight, Alison! Quite edible, ha-ha-ha! Pity I can't say the same for William, quite beats me why you stick to the same dreary outmoded man, year in, year out, surely it's time for some radical rethinking?'

'That's an honest question, James, and I shall do my best to answer it honestly. I know that's what people would expect of me. But that answer must be the same one I gave in 1963, and 1966, and again in 1970 and 1971, not to mention February of this year, when my ear-ring caught in your braces in the Stoke-Ribley's gazebo. William is fundamental to the philosophy in our marriage: you describe him as out-moded, I should prefer to describe him as traditional; what you call dreary, I would call honest. I think there's far too much experiment for its own sake these days. I appreciate that this somewhat conservative view may be unfashionable with younger marrieds, but, to put your question another way, if I may, I should like to . . .'

'I'm awfully sorry to cut you off, Alison, but that's all I have time for, I have to go across to Sylvia Clammering now where an early result is expected, so . . .'

'. . . ah, it seems to be risotto, Eric, Surely, that's something of a disappointment to you?'

'No, no, I should have preferred something a little more, how shall I put it, encouraging, but I assure you that I'm quite satisfied with the risotto.'

'Ha-ha-ha, well, I suppose you couldn't really be expected to say anything else, could you? And far be it from me to point out that before the buffet you were predicting anything from roast ptarmigan to *cochon de lait à la manière de la Comtesse de Virage!*'

'Look, Robin, I'm an old hand at this game, this isn't my first setback and God knows it won't be my last, but in this business you learn to be thankful for small mercies. It could have been a damn sight worse. It could have been fish fingers, or cheese and pineapple could have been . . .'

'. . . Felicity and Boris, sorry to grab you at a time like this, I know there are a thousand things you'd rather be doing, but it's a marvellous opportunity now that I've got you both together, and many of the guests are requiring some kind of statement from you, and I think they've a right to that statement tell me, how is it possible that the gin has run out?'

'Well, Gerald, I mean, that's not an easy, I mean, I'd require notice of that . . .'

'Perhaps I can answer for you Boris. The short answer, Gerald, is that people did not seem to like a claret cup. Now, I never pretend it would be a popular claret cup, but given the prevailing situation at the time, given the particular circumstances in which we found ourselves it was the only claret cup we could offer. I still maintain it was the right claret cup. But this is a democracy Gerald, the people have the right to choose, and they chose the gin. But I think you'll find that, as time goes on, they'll come round to our claret cup in the end. They're sensible people, basically, and they're good people, and they know that in the long run, what's right for us, what's right for the party, is right for them too. Does that answer your question?'

'Not entirely, but I can see that you've had enough for one evening and so . . .'

WILL FITZGERALD (activist)

Out campaigning one day, I knocked firmly on a door and stepped back, putting on my best candidate's face, only to have my smile wiped off immediately as the door fell off its hinges onto a horrified couple inside.

EDWINA CURRIE MP

The afternoon of the adoption meeting started well enough at a local school. I parked the big Citroen, my husband's pride and joy and lent to me only while my battered Austin was being serviced. I spent a happy hour inside at the meeting and returned – to find the car gone.

'Was that your big blue car which ran off down the road?' asked a lady. 'It ran down into Mr Theaker's garden and knocked down his wall,' she said helpfully. 'He's hopping mad.'

Down the road I went. It had started to rain. Mr Theaker was indeed standing in the demolished remains of his garden wagging his finger: 'Shan't vote for you,' he said. But where was the car? And what state was it in? Was I about to lose my husband's vote as well as Mr Theaker's?

And so to Swadlincote police station where three straight-faced sergeants solicitously asked about my relationship with my husband: 'Get on well, do you? That's lucky' . . . I was getting panicky and at last they took pity on me and escorted me to a nearby breaker's yard where the forlorn-looking car stood with but one headlight broken. The locals have been teasing me about this runaway start to our campaign ever since.

GREG KNIGHT MP

During election times, MPs wishing to retain their seats need a good memory for faces and names of their many workers. A few

MPs never admit that they haven't recognized a party faithful. One particular MP, therefore, said to the campaigner greeting him: 'Well, well, you have changed, Bill. You've lost weight, your hair has gone all grey and I see you don't wear glasses any more – oh, you've shaved off your beard as well. Crikey, Bill Jones, what on earth has happened?'

The man replied: 'I'm not Bill Jones, I'm Frederick Conway.'

'Good Heavens,' replied the MP, 'you've changed your name as well.'

PADDY ASHDOWN MP

Early in my political career I produced a leaflet (also an essential Liberal activity, incidentally) asking the good people of Yeovil to inform me if they lived in a council house and had problems with repairs. For three weeks my post bag was filled with returned reply forms, causing wry comments from the local postman, a boost to my wife's campaign to collect used stamps for some worthy cause or the other and a problem for me about what to do next.

I bravely (some would say foolishly) decided to visit all the complainants. It was winter, I recall, and bitterly cold when I made my sixth call of the evening on a house in one of our large council estates. Every one of my previous visits had insisted that I drink a cup of tea or coffee while the problem was explained (isn't it strange that only those who live in council houses invariably show such hospitality?). I was, in consequence, cross-legged with discomfort and desperately in need of relief, as they say in politer circles. As luck would have it my sixth problem involved a tap and a bathroom basin. I forget the precise nature of the defect, but it involved a great deal of demonstrative running of the tap. This made an unbearable situation imminently cata-strophic as far as I was concerned. I stopped my complainant in mid-flow, explained my predicament and begged to be excused for a moment, *in lieu.* After he'd gone I made full use of the facility standing temptingly in the corner of the room.

It was, I suspect, the sheer joy of relief which caused me to pull the chain afterwards with more than my customary vigour. Whatever the cause, however, the large, cast iron cistern (marked 'Shanks' as I recall and clearly built to last 1000 years) chose this moment of its thirty-year life to detach itself from the wall and crash to the floor.

My complainant, who had asked me in about a mere faulty tap, arrived on the scene very quickly and, amid the water, broken pipe and scattered plaster, enquired whether or not I was now about to ask him if he would vote Liberal as well.

BOB PARSONS (activist)

Before I went canvassing for a parish election in a small Hertfordshire village, I took the precaution of asking the candidate what issues he was standing up for. Hearing nothing remotely controversial I was greatly heartened, and when the first would-be voter asked what the candidate would do for the village if elected, I replied confidently: 'He's going to try to install a new lighting system.'

'Oh, he is, is he? Well, he's not getting my vote, I want the rural nature of the village preserved.'

STAN CROWTHER MP

During my by-election in 1976, two of the full-time organizers who had been drafted in were given the job of erecting boards bearing 'Vote Labour' posters in front gardens.

So many residents responded positively to their overtures that they quickly ran out of wood. Showing the initiative always associated with Labour Party organizers, they began scouring derelict sites for scrap wood. Arriving at what appeared to be a slum clearance site, they saw a row of apparently empty houses and the usual row of outside WCs at the back. Overjoyed by the discovery of this splendid source of raw material, they started ripping off the lavatory doors. They were about half way through the task when they pulled off a door and found an old lady sitting on the throne.

I never did find out whether she voted Labour.

JERRY HAYES MP

During the by-election in Portsmouth South I went to canvass on behalf of the Conservative candidate, Patrick Rock. After a heavy day of canvassing I finished up by banging on a door in a block

Mahood's Guide to Electioneering

(Punch, 20 February 1974)

TRY AND CATCH THE FLOATING VOTER

'Follow that car!'

TRY AND GAUGE THE MOOD OF YOUR MEETING

'Communists, extremists, militants . . . testing.'

TELL THEM THE OLD, OLD STORY

'Could you drop in a few quotes from Enoch?
You're not rousing our rabble!'

of flats. After a few moments, the door was opened and I was greeted by the tallest woman I have ever seen in my life, and what is more, she was as broad as she was tall. Halfway through my patter, it suddenly occurred to me that this woman had five o'clock shadow. To my horror it suddenly dawned on me that this was no woman, but a man dressed up. It was at this point that my smooth politician's patter completely went to pieces, and all I could stammer to the individual was 'Can you tell me – are you a Conservative?' The reply was as honest as it was interesting: 'To be perfectly frank, I'm not sure what I am.'

6
Public Meetings and Other Accidents

IAIN DALE (PA to Patrick Thompson MP)

Recently, I started doing talks for 'Peace Through Nato' and my first one was for a school in Orpington. I was extremely nervous, not having done this type of thing for some time but my nervousness was compounded when I sat down and the chair promptly collapsed leaving me sprawling on the floor. The chair had obviously unilaterally disarmed itself. But at least the audience fell in with my ideas.

A. CECIL WALKER MP

A well-known religious politican was finishing his campaign address by requesting his listeners to vote for him when a man jumped up angrily to his feet and shouted: 'I'd rather vote for the devil.'

'Quite so,' said the politician with a smile, 'but in case your friend declines to run, may I count on your support?'

ROGER WALLACE (Labour activist)

At a crucial by-election our candidate was the last to speak. The other two had been lambasting a trade union which didn't have a postal ballot but which had recently gone on strike.

Our man stood firm and straight. 'In fact,' he said, looking fiercely at his political opponents, 'they haven't got their facts straight. That trade union *did* have a postal ballot.' His supporters went wild and the evening was a great success from our point of view.

Later, in the car, I said to him: 'Did they really have a postal ballot?'

'Buggered if I know,' he retorted.

MALCOLM RIFKIND MP

A few years ago when I was speaking in Scotland for one of our candidates in the European Elections, the chairman of a public meeting got up and said to the audience: 'We are delighted to welcome Mr Rifkind. We often hear that Mr Rifkind is going places and I just want to say the quicker he goes the better!'

BOB EDWARDS MP

My father-in-law, Elijah Sandham, who was the first Labour MP for Kirkdale, stood at a by-election for the local council in Chorley where there were very few WCs. At a public meeting one of the speakers said: 'There are too many privvies in this town and too few water closets. What we want on the council is someone to get stuck into them, someone like Elijah Sandham.'

JO RICHARDSON MP

I was a nervous young candidate and sat waiting while Harold Wilson and other major figures made their speeches. Right at the end of the meeting, I was called to an encouraging round of applause.

I took a step forward and then – horror! I could feel my French knickers start to slowly fall down my thighs and around my ankles.

Not sure what to do or who might have seen, I stepped sideways and with my left foot, swept them deftly under the table. It didn't help to steady me down with that huge audience, but at least I was quick on the drawers!

JULIAN AMERY MP

In 1950, I was fighting the General Election and having my honeymoon at the same time.

The campaign itself was tense and we knew it would be a close run thing. But all the world loves a young couple and Catherine's presence on my platform swung many votes to me. At one meeting, in our worst ward, an old-fashioned type of working man, unshaven and wearing a scarf and cloth cap, asked me what time I got up in the morning. I answered that I rose at eight. He shouted back: 'Eight? You lazy bastard. Why, I get up at five every morning.'

Another man of much the same type got up two rows behind. He turned to his mate and, pointing at Catherine, said to him: 'Yer wouldn't if yer went to bed with yon.'

KAY LINDLEY (activist)

During the SDP Conference in Bradford, my son Richard, then aged three, approached Shirley Williams and tapped her on the behind to ask: 'Do you love me?'

Whereupon Shirley (a politician to the end) replied: 'Well, if I knew you better, I might.'

MALCOLM RIFKIND MP

I was speaking to the constituency association of a fellow MP. The chairman had been correctly informed that my constituency is called Edinburgh, Pentlands. However, he seemed to get confused and when he rose to introduce me insisted on referring to me as the Member for Penthouse. I replied that I wished I were.

TONY BENN MP

On an election platform in Taunton in 1956 the chairman made two comments that have stuck in my mind. First he said:

> 'Sir Anthony Eden has been to Washington and has issued a declaration there. He did not have to go to Washington to issue that declaration. Anybody could have written it.'

He then looked round the platform and glancing at me he said:

> 'Why, Tony Benn could have written it. It was full of platitudes.'

Later he introduced the candidate Reg Pestell, as:

'The weapon with which on Thursday we shall strike a blow at Great Britain.'

JOHN WATSON MP

In early December a couple of years ago I was invited to speak to a local Conservative branch's annual general meeting. I mentioned to the chairman that December was an unusual time for an AGM. He agreed. 'We did have a meeting in October but only six people turned up so we decided to hold it again tonight with a bit of incentive for people to come.'

'I see,' I said, 'and is that why I am your speaker tonight?'

'No, it's not. We've laid on some crisps and a meat pie.'

'Can I place an order for an Election party, sale or return?'

ROBERT MAXWELL (Publisher, Mirror Group Newspapers)

In 1964 I was the Labour candidate for North Bucks, and on the eve of the poll I was addressing a packed meeting in Bletchley. A number of Tories were noisily heckling, and the calls arose:

'Don't vote for Maxwell – he's a foreigner.'
'You are a Czech!'

I replied, 'So that is what the Tory canvassers tell you. Well, let me say that I came to this country with a rifle in my hand. What is more, I am at least as British as His Royal Highness Prince Philip, and as far as I am aware both the Queen and the country are very happy with his service!' Picking out the chief heckler, I continued:

'Where were you born?'
'In England, whereas you were only naturalized!'
'Tell me when you were born did you have to make any effort?'
'Of course not!'
'Well did you have to make a choice about where to be born?'
'No!'
'Well, sir, I did both. I chose this country, and I made an effort to come here because it's the finest in the world.'

The audience of some 2000, over half of whom were Tory, was totally convinced and gave me a standing ovation. As I left the hall, the Chairman of one of the major Tory branches furtively pushed an envelope into my hand. On opening it later, I found a note saying:

'Congratulations – you deserve to win.'

And I did.

LADY EYRE

How do you follow this introduction to your after-dinner speech: 'Anyone who has never heard Sir Reginald Eyre speak before, will be looking forward to hearing him. I am sure you will enjoy his debatable qualities and find his speech as moving as the food has been.'

GEOFF LAWLER MP

After-dinner speech:

A candidate's life involves going to many such dinners as this: for example, last week I was speaking at the Bradford Haemorrhoid Sufferers Society – a stand-up buffet; the week before it was the Bolton Naturists Group; the week before that it was the Gay Rugby League and prior to that the Eccleshill Ex-Convicts Association. So I apologise to those of you who have heard this speech four times already.

ANONYMOUS

Demosthenes used to say it with pebbles, but I am envious of the politician who said he could get away with the same speech on the same day by taking his teeth out for one of them.

MICHAEL BLOND

Having given a particularly long speech, a pompous parliamentary candidate berated his PA: 'Dammit Smith, I asked you to write me a 20-minute speech and the thing went on for a whole hour.' To which his puzzled PA replied: 'But I did write you a 20-minute speech . . .' Then, after a moment's thought: 'And I attached two carbon copies.'

LORD ONGROW

A famous politician found only one person present at a farmers' meeting he was due to address. Wondering whether to proceed, he asked the audience who said: 'If I had only one hen, I would feed it.' The politician duly made an erudite, complete and masterly speech and then enquired if the farmer had enjoyed it. 'Aye,' said the farmer, 'but if I'd had only one hen, I wouldn't have given it a bucketful.'

SIR JOHN BIGGS-DAVIDSON MP

The nervous parliamentary candidate asked advice about speech-making from a senior MP. 'I try to make 'em laugh,' said the experienced man. 'I often start like this: "Some of the happiest times of my life have been spent in the arms of another man's wife." Then, in the shocked silence, I wait a few seconds and say: "I refer of course, to my mother." '

The candidate started his next speech very well. 'Some of the happiest times of my life have been spent in the arms of another man's wife.' He waited a few seconds . . . then a few seconds more. Finally, he blurted out: 'But I'm damned if I can remember who she was.'

'I think I blew it!'

SIR KENNETH LEWIS MP

A voter, asked what the local parliamentary candidate's speech was like replied: 'A bit like an ox's head. Two good points and a lot of bull in between.'

JOHN TOMLINSON MEP

During a debate on artificial insemination a British member was speaking eloquently about the 'moral and ethical problems of the use of frozen semen'. Imagine the blank looks on the faces of German MEPs when in German translation they got the equivalent of the 'moral and ethical problems of extremely cold sailors'.

JOE HAINES (Group Political Editor, Mirror Group Newspapers)

I was in Glasgow during the general election campaign of 1964. The star speaker at a Labour rally was George Brown. The chairman introduced him thus:

'I've had a worrd with Mr Broon. He tells me he's nae gonna make a long speech and he's nae gonna make a short speech. He's gonna make a mediocre speech.'

JOHN MACKAY MP

One of the funnier incidents which happened to me was when I visited a Hall in my constituency for an election meeting. At the back of the Hall for quite obvious reasons, right beside the main light switch there was a notice which said 'Please switch off the lights before leaving the Hall.'

Someone had, of course, decorated the room with some 'John MacKay' election posters and had put one of them up without too much care (at least I hope without too much care). And as I stood up to speak I was faced with 'Please switch off John MacKay before leaving the Hall.'

CYRIL NOTTINGHAM (activist)

I was at a public meeting up north recently where a Tory junior minister was being heckled. The rather pompous Tory, a southerner threatened: 'Sir if you don't shut up, I'll pick you up and put you in my pocket.'

Came the prompt reply: 'Thee'll have more brains in thy pocket than thee has in thy head, then.'

PAMELA JOLLY (activist)

At an election public meeting the-then MP for St Albans, Victor Goodhew, was asked a question about Suez.

'That's rather an old fish,' said Mr Goodhew.
'Yes and it still stinks,' said his constituent.

DAVID MADEL MP

One of my favourite stories is that of a certain politician addressing an election meeting, when a member of the audience stood up and said, 'I would not vote for you if you were the Archangel Gabriel', to which the speaker replied, 'My dear sir, if I were the Archangel Gabriel you would not be living in my constituency.'

LORD CLEDWYN

At a packed meeting in North Wales, a male heckler yelled at Megan Lloyd-George: 'Don't you wish you were a man?' and Megan Lloyd-George yelled back: 'Don't you wish you were?'

7

Who Goes There?

ROBIN SQUIRE MP

Calling on a small cottage, the door was answered by the lady of the house, who made the depressing and still fairly common comment, 'You don't want me, you want my husband.' She disappeared, and shortly afterwards a man mountain who looked as if he'd discovered the secret of fire the previous week, arrived to confront me, with a growing growl. He proceeded to shout, 'You Conservatives are the biggest, nastiest, meanest group of tricksters that has ever been in any Government in this country.' I was about to write him down as a doubtful when he suddenly said, 'But wait a minute – aren't you Robin Squire?' Visibly raising myself another six inches after his earlier tirade, and seeing some prospect of deliverance from his otherwise all-embracing damnation, I piped up smilingly, 'Yes, I am.'

'And you're the meanest, nastiest, worst of the lot!!!!!!'

IAN AITKEN (Political Editor, *The Guardian*)

Sir Walter Clegg, Tory MP for Wyre, went canvassing with his team in a particular street. He was somewhat taken aback when the front door was half-opened and a voice said defensively: 'Not today, thank you.'

The second door, and another wary voice: 'Kindly go away.' The third said: 'Bugger off. We don't want any of your muck here.'

Only later did he discover that a horse manure salesman had been round pushing leaflets through letterboxes saying he would be round that afternoon.

JULIA LANGDON (Political Editor, *Sunday Mirror*)

Denis Healey was out canvassing in the market place in the Ryedale by-election when he ran into one of the few remaining people in Britain who did not actually appear to recognize him.

'Don't you know who I am?' asked Denis, with a little hurt indignation behind his best, bluff Yorkshire manner.

'No,' said the innocent voter. 'I'm blind.'

Denis was not deterred. 'Well, don't you recognize my voice, then?' he demanded. 'No,' she said. 'I don't.'

Whereupon Old Eyebrows took hold of one of her hands and guided it to his face and his most famous feature. 'Oh,' she cried. 'You're Denis Healey!'

JOHN WARDEN (Political Editor, *Daily Express*)

Down in Croydon, when canvassing as a Tory candidate, the Speaker, Mr Bernard Weatherill, was obliged to converse through the letter-box with a householder who refused to open the door. From the background came a voice, 'Who is it, Edna?'

'Bleedin' gypsies,' replied Edna, snapping the letterbox shut.

Candidates often despair at how little of their message really sinks in, even when they are permitted to speak. Nicholas Fairbairn tells how in one campaign in Scotland he would give his very cogent and moving doorstep speech and, immediately behind, a Tory back-up team of helpers would follow on to consolidate his gains. In theory it was like shelling peas.

They came to one house and asked the occupant if someone had called.

'Yes,' she said. 'There was a chap. Selling bibles, I think.'

PATRICK JENKIN MP

The dialogue needs to be spoken in a rather precise, Aberdeenshire Scottish accent which gets broader with each repetition.

The man went up the path to the old lady's front door with his collecting tin.

'I'm from the Aberdeen, Arbroath and Kirkaldy Agricultural Co-operative Old Comrades Association Brass Band Instrumental Renewal Fund,' he announced.

'Eh?' said the old lady.

(A little louder) 'I'm from the Aberdeen, Arbroath and Kirkaldy Agricultural Co-operative Old Comrades Association Brass Band Instrumental Renewal Fund.'

'I'm a bit hard o' hearing!' shouted the lady.

(More slowly and much louder:) 'I'm from the Aberdeen, Arbroath and Kirkaldy Agricultural Co-operative Old Comrades Association Brass Band Instrumental Renewal Fund.'

'Eh? I canna hear ye!'

'Och, to Hell wi' ye!' and he stalked off down the path.

'Aye,' said the old lady, 'and to Hell wi' ye, too, *and* the Aberdeen, Arbroath and Kirkaldy Agricultural Co-operative Old Comrades Association Brass Band Instrumental Renewal Fund.'

MARJORIE PROOPS

I was trudging around the streets of Grimsby with Austin Mitchell during his 1977 campaign. It was cold, of course, (I have *no* warm memories of trudging around streets anywhere on sunny summery days). Austin strode purposefully and knocked on doors vigorously while I drooped and shivered at his heels. It was early afternoon and almost all the doors were opened by housewives. Some were smartly slammed shut again but mostly there was a welcome on a lot of mats for Austin. And on one mat in particular for me.

The lady ignored the hopeful candidate but she grabbed my arm and manoeuvred me past him into her warm parlour. 'It's my old man,' she said, and for the next hour or so graphically described their difficulties, which were not of a political nature. It was dark when at last I emerged, after a counselling session. Austin had disappeared. He went on to glory, and I often wonder if the same may be said of the complainant's husband.

J. E. HUTTON (Belfast)

A little boy answered the door while I was out canvassing one evening. 'Can you come back next week?' he said. 'Only my mother is on the phone.'

SIR GEOFFREY JOHNSON-SMITH MP

The door opened in answer to my knock and I told the man: 'I'm here to see if you'll be supporting the Tory candidate.'

'Is that "Tory" you said?' he asked in an Irish accent.

'Yes, that's right.'

The man exploded. 'Do you know how your party got its name? It's called after Captain Tory, an Englishman who plundered Ireland. Plunderers you've been and plunderers you are.'

I made a tactical withdrawal.

'Come elections, I'd choose Alaric:
He looks like a Vandal, talks like a
Vandal, acts like a Vandal.'

GREVILLE JANNER MP

I have the only hereditary seat there has ever been in the Labour Party. My late father, Barnett – later Lord Janner of the City of Leicester – was MP for my part of Leicester until 1970. He was forced out of the 1970 election campaign due to severe ill health and on doctor's orders.

Like bees around the political honeypot, suitors for the seat wooed the local party. After a bitter battle, I was eventually selected as candidate. I have given up denying the marvellous legend that the Party had no alternative other than to accept me because the posters had already been printed with JANNER FOR LEICESTER NORTH WEST on them, and they could not afford a reprint with another name!

From then on, I have campaigned in successive elections with the slogan JANNER CARES. In 1983, I took an elderly lady to the poll and she said: 'Don't worry, Barney, I have always voted for you and I'm not going to stop now!'

At a local Working Men's Club, I was presented as follows: 'I have no need to introduce your Labour candidate, whose name is a household word – Sir Bernard Granner!'

Still: among my happiest times were those when I was in the Commons and Father was still in the Lords. I treasure a letter from a man who was a constituent of each of us in turn and who was not quite sure which had been elected and was certainly taking no chances. It is addressed to 'Lord Greville Janner MP, House of Commons'. It starts: 'Dear Sir or Madam'!

JULIA LANGDON (Political Editor, *Daily Mirror*)

When a friend stood for Kensington and Chelsea Council (successfully) in 1974, she advanced on a front door and the man of the house listened to her bit; 'I'm from the Labour Party, hope we can count on you, etc.' and then he said: 'From the Labour Party eh? Well, I've got a complaint!' She looked quickly at her voters' register and said: 'A complaint?'

'Yes – about the local nursery school.'

For fifteen minutes, he expounded and she listened.

'Right,' she said finally. 'I'll make a note of your complaint – Mr . . . ?'

'Portnoy,' he answered. And so it was that my friend could say in all honesty, that she had experienced a Portnoy's Complaint!

WILLIAM WILSON (County Councillor)

Harold Wilson was of course party leader in 1964 and I went to one house canvassing. An old man came to the door and I told him my name was Wilson and I was the Labour candidate. He looked at me a bit carefully and said 'You don't look very much like you do on the television but I think you'll make a good Prime Minister.'

PETER THURNHAM MP

I first stood for election as a local councillor in May 1982. I had been approached at very short notice on the day that nominations went in, to stand in an area where I was a complete stranger. I managed to canvass nearly every house in the ward, and at the election, won with the largest majority of the night. Behind this apparently undiluted tale of success and bravado, there lies a very different story.

The local party workers were reluctant to help with canvassing, and there was no literature available to help me, apart from some small roneoed cards which said, 'Sorry you were out when I called, Peter Thurnham'.

As I sat in my car utterly terrified to go out and meet anyone, it occurred to me that if I watched carefully when people left their houses, I could then slip in one of these cards, and never have to actually meet any of the electorate!

JOHN WARDEN (Political Editor, *Daily Express*)

The most discreet doorstep brush-off to any political activist came from a woman who cut the canvasser short with an apology.

'You see,' she said. 'My husband and I don't indulge.'

ROBIN SQUIRE MP

On the last Saturday of the campaign, I was sharing a microphone in my High Street with a dashing, debonair, blond-haired, good-speaking (do I sound sufficiently jealous?) non-Parliamentary, male campaigner. As chance would have it, whilst he was on the microphone he was spotted by two young women, and comments were uttered along the lines of 'He's a bit of alright!' and 'Corrrr! I wouldn't mind voting for 'im.' My wife, who was standing beside them, being anxious to correct any misunderstanding, said 'Oh no, he's not the candidate – that man over there is the candidate and he's also my husband.' Greeting this news with all the enthusiasm normally afforded Dracula in a blood bank, the young women walked away.

GRAHAM SMITH (agent)

Whilst canvassing for the 'Keep Britain in Europe' campaign as a rather new Young Conservative, I was becoming increasingly depressed when, one lunchtime, all my appeals for support were seemingly falling on deaf ears. Imagine my pleasure, then, when

I discovered that the father of one of my best friends was to be the next house call of the day.

'Good afternoon, *Mr Fisher*', I said with mock formality and a smile beaming from one side of my face to the other. 'I'm calling on behalf of the "Keep Britain in Europe" campaign and I hope we can rely on your support.'

Mr Fisher, who seemed to be enjoying a mouthful of his lunch whilst on the doorstep, replied: 'Ah, now then . . . let me see . . . what's your name?'

'Graham Smith,' I replied eagerly, entering into the spirit of the joke and thinking perhaps he knew me but couldn't remember my name.

'And where do you live?' he continued.

'23 Sparkford Close, Mr Fisher,' I continued, still grinning.

'And have you ever seen me knocking on your door?' he asked.

'I don't think so, Mr Fisher . . .'

'Well,' he replied, 'Don't ******** well come knocking on mine!'

And with that, he slammed the door.

LADY FALKENDER (former top aide to Harold Wilson)

When Harold Wilson, then Prime Minister, was on an election tour visit to Glasgow, the Lord Provost came to pay his respects. The suite of rooms was decorated in the style then fashionable, of papering the cupboards and doors exactly the same as the walls. The staff were on parade to meet all the distinguished visitors. With great dignity, I left the room to find some papers for the Prime Minister, only to discover that I had entered a walk-in cupboard. I was far too embarrassed to re-appear so I stayed in the cupboard until the Lord Provost had left.

BEN PATTERSON MEP

In the first European elections of 1979 Shelagh Roberts (now Dame) came top of the poll in London South West. But it turned out that there had been an irregularity and the election had to be held all over again. Conservative Members of the European Parliament duly turned up for the by-election to lend her their support.

A group of us MEPs arrived at party headquarters in Putney

to the consternation of the transport officer from Conservative Central Office. Who were we all? he asked.

Consulting his movement sheet he found that, indeed, he had been due at that time to pick up one – but only one – visitor: a certain 'Mr M. E. Peas'.

ALF DUBS MP

When I was canvassing in Battersea during the election campaign, I rang the doorbell of a multi-occupied house and a lady and a small child of about four came to the door. I did not know who she was as the doorbells did not have names on them. When I stated my business, however, she shut the door in my face. As I was deciding whether to mark her down as 'against' or 'doubtful', to my delight the door opened once again – no doubt she had been to turn the kettle off – and I was about to relaunch my campaign in a more confident vein, when the lady turned to the small child. 'You see,' she said, chastising it gently. 'I told you there was nothing to see. It's only a politician.'

IVOR GABER (activist)

In the pub after the selection conference, a Labour activist was very disappointed that he wasn't chosen to fight the seat. 'Well,' said someone who'd taken part in the procedure, 'you didn't get chosen because you're Australian.'

'I'm not,' said the activist, surprised.

'Well, you have an Australian accent.'

The activist thought for a moment. 'That does it. From now on, I'll give up the Cockney accent and admit that I went to Charterhouse.'

MICHAEL LORD MP

On canvassing round Willow Walk, I came across a huge bouquet of flowers propped up against a front door. Correctly assuming the occupant to be out, I put a 'Sorry you were out when I called' card through the letterbox.

Next morning, a delightful note came for me at party headquarters: 'Mrs White of 26 Willow Walk is sorry she was out when

you called but thank you for the beautiful flowers and of course
I will be voting for you.'

JOHN GOLDING MP

I was out canvassing and at one door had this exchange with a
voter:
    'I'm John Golding, your Labour candidate.'
    'No you're not.'
    'Yes I am.'
    'No you're not – he's tall and good-looking.'
For the record, I am 5 ft 6 ins tall. I hope this clears up any
misunderstanding.

Campaign Charlies

(Punch, 18 May 1983)

MICHAEL BYWATER

Talking of the General Election, I've actually met the most important
people in British politics. Saatchi, I mean, and Saatchi. I once worked
for the most extraordinary bore who conceived in his megalomania the
idea of hiring them to prop up the crumbling public image of his
appalling company. Both Saatchis came to one of those stupid
meetings at which nothing is achieved and the only thing that happens
is that one is 'in' it. ('I'm sorry, caller, he's in a . . .')
    One Saatchi wore specs but the other one didn't. They were bright
and eager and natty and kept pulling bits of paper out of their
burgundy leather briefcases and waving them at us. This impressed
the extraordinary bore, but not me, and as the Saatchis were leaving,
I murmured to them, 'Thank you for auditioning. *We'll let you know.'*
    I wouldn't say they blanched at my impertinence, but they certainly
wobbled a bit around the edges, and rang up later to say they didn't
fancy the job because the money wasn't enough.
    Well, it all sorted itself out in the wash. The extraordinary bore is
now very rich and opens his house to the public twice a year; and I
got the sack, my fiscal career subsequently being limited to letters
from old-established Chancery solicitors begging to advise that
previously-unknown uncles in Australia have disinherited me.
    And Saatchi and Saatchi are doing jolly well, depending on what you
mean by 'doing jolly well'; and whatever it means it cannot possibly
encompass the Conservative Party Political Broadcast I heard on the

wireless the other day, a ghastly harbinger of miseries to come in the run-up to the General Election.

Perhaps you didn't hear it, but what we got was a sort of hideous duff parody of Gilbert and Sullivan performed by a croaking atonal chorus of Equity rejects accompanied by a one-armed, possibly dead, pianist, with a refrain which went:

So it's thumbs down to

Layb-uh, Lib'ral and the Ess Dee Pee and, in the interstices, an oily voice-over cracking pathetic little jokes like: 'And now, industry leaves the stage, driven off by the nasty Labour Rates Rises . . . and, alas, taking a number of jobs with it as they go in search of a Conservative-controlled council.' Brief pause for the stupid bovine electorate to laugh sycophantically and blow its brains out in excitement, and then plonkety-plonk-plink-plunk from the Ted Heath sound-alike at the ivories, and back to the bloody silly chorus again.

The whole thing reeked of contempt, though how anyone capable of writing feeble bilge like that can feel contemptuous of anyone is beyond me. Presumably they think it's the kind of stuff that worthy stolid Black Country Ironmasters, laden with Victorian Values, will like, though one would have thought that anyone with *any* values would more likely respond with a bar of white-hot pig-iron up the Manifesto.

I wondered at first what they thought they were playing at, apart from silly buggers, but then it became obvious. This was ad-men's stuff. Associate the product with pleasurable sensations (e.g., Gilbert and Sullivan) rather than unpleasurable ones (e.g., the dole queue) and the punters will rush to the polling booths full of goodwill. You can imagine the ghastly ad-men's conversation:

(The offices of Shifty & Shifty, purveyors of tall stories, fine conceits and unverifiable propositions. Seated at a scarlet perspex table, wittily lit from below by neon votive candles, are Malcolm, Biff and Jules. Malcolm is dressed in a lightweight dove-grey suit, Harvie & Hudson striped shirt and blue polka-dot tie. Biff is dressed in a lightweight dove-grey suit, Harvie & Hudson striped shirt and blue polka-dot tie. Jules is on the creative side, so is wearing a viridian flock tracksuit, aquamarine running shoes and witty tee-shirt. Malcolm is tapping on the table with a gold pen. So is Biff. Jules is tapping on the table with a Rotring drawing pen, because he is on the creative side.)

Malcolm: What we want is something nice.

Biff: Something friendly, light.

Jules: Upbeat.

Biff: Upmarket.

Malcolm: Not *too* upbeat.

Jules: Not *too* upmarket.

Biff: Middle-of-the-road.

Malcolm: No politics.

Biff: No policies.

Jules: Just middle-of-the-road.

Malcolm: How about this?

Jules: Run it up the flagpole.

Biff: Put it on the step.

Jules: See if anyone salutes it.

Biff: See if the cat licks it.

Malcolm: It's just a thought.

Jules: Toss it in.

Biff: Kick it around.

(They go back to the beginning and repeat themselves until lunchtime, whereupon all parties fade out and aren't seen again until they wake up at 2.00 a.m. in their secretaries' beds.)

All rather unsubtle, if you ask me, liable to backfire, and not just because to many of us Gilbert and Sullivan is the musical equivalent of watching the washing go round in the launderette. There are, after all, a large number of human activities which have pleasant associations but we aren't going to be inspired to vote Alliance by, say, a witty little television filmette of David Steel doing it to Shirley Williams, even if he does wear a label saying 'Tories' and she one saying 'Britain'. Too, too Hogarthian, my dear, but not the right way at all.

Same thing goes for William Whitelaw dressed as The Laughing Policeman and singing the hilarious Police and Criminal Justice Bill words:

And as I pound my lonely beat
While you are all in bed
I'll see a Black Man in the street
And bash him in the head (using the powers of arrest proposed by the Conservative Party).
CHORUS
Hahahahahahahahahahahaha AAGH
Haaah, hahahahahahahaha BANG.

Can you imagine Churchill going in for that sort of rubbish? Of course not. He used to potter into shot, stare with deep suspicion into the lens for a bit, and then go into a speech, with long words about policies, and rhodomontade, and all rest of the rhetorical rattle which made politics such fun before the current Keep Politics Out of Politics movement began to emerge, last week. You can't see the the boy going on television drenched in baked beans, because some advertising psychologist has told him people like baked beans and . . .

. . . We interrupt this joke to bring you a Party Political Broadcast on behalf of the Labour Party.
(A field. The Worzel Gummidge *theme tune. Angle on Michael Foot strapped to a stick with a crow on his head. Slowly, he falls over into the mud, still strapped to his stick, which, we see, is labelled 'constituency selection committees'.)*
Foot: *(Through a mouthful of bull's doings)* You may think this is what'd happen to Britain if Labour get in. You may be right. But nothing's certain. Mrs Thatcher's policies of so-called economic recovery aren't working. So we in the Labour *(suddenly shouting)* PARTY HAVE DECIDED NOT TO *(reverts to 'normal' voice)* have any policies of recovery. This may sound odd. But it is. The price of vigilance is eternal freedom. Fee-fi-fo . . .
(A tractor labelled 'Benn' comes into shot dragging a plough labelled 'Militant Tendency'. It ploughs Foot under, and immediately sheaves of golden corn spring up, labelled 'True Socialism'. Enter a chorus of dancing rhizomes, lesbians and Roman Catholic clergymen, in a lambent aurora of exploding prejudices and crystalline absurdities, singing the famous 'Loonies' Gavotte' from Heseltine and Saatchi's opera, Care Opportunities for Graduates. *Everything goes black, under the auspices of the CRE.)*
　　Well, we shall see. The corridors of power will be reeking of aftershave over the next few weeks as silly young men and silly young politicians rush around coming up with "creative" ideas and giving off a disagreeable redolence of rancid butter or old peas in their fervour ('For God's *sake,* Adrian, where can we find a wide-angle lens big enough to get all of Cyril in at once?') and never even suspecting that we're not as stupid as we think they are.
　　'Lights! Camera speed! And . . . ACTION.' Oh, oh, oh. Hee hee hee hee, oh stop it, stop it, ha ha ha ha, oh, you're killing me, oh dear no ha ha *(falls over and clutches belly, too exhausted with laughter to go out and vote).*

RON BROWN MP (LEITH)

When I was first elected in 1979, I stayed in a small Pimlico hotel. Unfortunately the owner was very inquisitive. He obviously wondered about my strange hours and bundle of papers. Every so often he would ask what I did. Wishing for a quiet life, I always parried the question. One day, his patience running out, he asked me straight out about my job.

　　'Oh,' I said, 'I am an engineer,' referring to my original occupation.

'Oh,' he said, 'only I thought you might be a VAT man . . .'
Evidently doubt still gnawed at his innards because I learnt that
he emigrated to Australia shortly afterwards.

DAVID ALTON MP (Lib)

During the last general election, I took part in a number of early
morning (dawn chorus) leaflet drops which have always seemed
to me to be the ultimate test of the power of political conviction
over common sense. On one particular morning, still groggy with
tiredness, I had just put one leaflet through the letter slot, and
accidentally kicked a bottle of milk, upsetting the contents all
over the doorstep.

What to do? Waking the household up at 6 o'clock in the
morning to apologise would undoubtedly sour the situation for
the Liberal Party altogether. A scribbled note on a leaflet under
the empty bottle might do the trick but, of course, dressing in
semi-darkness I'd forgotten my pen. The only thing I could do
was to leave two ten-pence pieces under the bottle and make my
escape before I did any more damage.

Later on in the day, while canvassing in the same area, a lady
came up to me and explained that it was her pint of milk and that
a neighbour had seen the whole incident. I braced myself for the
inevitable onslaught. To my astonishment, she told me that she
was a staunch Conservative 'and always would be' but, because
of the 10 pence pieces, this time she'd vote Liberal!

8
Democracy Calling

PAUL EDDINGTON

Odd things have been happening to me since we started to show
Yes Minister world-wide.

The first time I visited Australia was in 1983 on the eve of a
general election. My host said would I like to meet the Prime
Minister, Malcolm Fraser? We went down to the Regent Hotel
in Sydney to find the ballroom packed with Liberal Party
supporters. I was introduced to various senior party members and
then Mr Fraser and his entourage came in. I was led up on to the
platform. The Prime Minister and I were chatting away pleasantly
when I heard it being announced that I would be making the first
speech. In spite of the midsummer heat my feet suddenly went
icy. I felt I had only two options: to faint away and be carried
out (I imagined the headlines, 'Minister Tired and Emotional,'
'Minister Succumbs to Jet Lag,') or to make a speech.

I stepped to the rostrum, in front of which was the nation's
press corps and several TV cameras. I explained that if I were to
express a political preference I should probably be deported, and
possibly summoned before the Director General of the BBC on
my return, so I had decided to nail my colours firmly to the fence.
I could however make a prediction about the outcome of the
election. The Liberal Party held it's collective breath. The winner
would not be our host of that evening. Silence in the ballroom.
Nor would it be Bob Hawke, the Labour Leader. The winner
would undoubtedly be, I said, the Civil Service. Relief all round
– not least from myself!

DAVID HARRIS MP (Cons)

Before the last General Election, I went down the Geevor Tin
Mine in my constituency to do a bit of underground canvassing.
After a long walk along one of the lower levels, we came across
two Cornish miners drilling an ore lode. Shouting above the noise,
the Deputy Manager introduced me. One of the miners gave a
thumbs up sign. The other spat. I reckoned that if I got 50 percent
of the miners' vote, I wouldn't be doing badly.

Punch, 16 October 1974

'The election was, for once, surprisingly accurate,' said Herbert
Sample, head of Opinion Test, after it was all over. 'In 1970 and again
in February this year, the election results were dangerously misleading.
We had shown that the real opinion of the country was Labour, then
Tory; but the few percent inaccuracy of the crude election voting
system actually got the wrong government in power. This time, the
election results chose the same side as the polls. It's amazing, really.
We ask a series of sophisticated and elaborate questions, designed
to sift out all possible error. *They* simply ask the sample to put an X
on a bit of paper. What surprises me is not how accurate the Election
is, but that they get anywhere near our figures at all.'

ERIC COCKERAM MP

On a dark and wintry night in the late 1940s I was a young
Conservative canvassing in Birkenhead, ringing the bell at the
impressive home of Miss Laird (of Cammell Laird Shipbuilding).
The door was answered by an elderly maid with a white linen cap
and apron. I explained that I was canvassing on behalf of the
Conservatives but before I could get any further there was a shout
from the background – 'Who is it Nellie?' 'It's the Conservatives
Ma'am,' came the reply, followed by the appearance of Miss Laird
herself.

I again explained the purpose of my call and was assured of her
support. I then said that on my canvass list was a 'Miss Nellie
O'Brien' and I wondered if we could rely on *her* support. Nellie
was about to return to the bowels of the kitchen but a fierce shout
froze her in her tracks, 'Nellie – you're Conservative aren't you,'
said her Mistress rhetorically. 'Yes Ma'am,' mumbled Nellie

obsequiously. I thanked Miss Laird, Nellie barred the door, and I put a firm cross in the 'doubtful' column.

J. S. SCRUTON (activist)

One Election Day when I was 'knocking up' and collecting supporters by car to take them to vote, I arrived at the garden gate of one house at the identical moment as my opposite number from a rival party. We marched up the path together. 'I think you've made a mistake,' he said rather icily, as he rung the doorbell. I replied: 'I think you'll find the mistake is yours.'

The lady of the house came to the door. My rival and I stood silently side by side as she glanced at our rosettes. 'I'm yours,' she said, looking at me, and those words, even spoken with a rather different implication, never sounded sweeter!

MICK LUCKHURST (election aide)

Our candidate, whom I drove throughout the General Election, had a catchy jingle which we played constantly through the loudspeaker. Outside a school one day, the music carousing merrily, he was greeting mums and I was guarding the car. Suddenly I was aware of the car rocking violently. Around the other side of it, a man in pyjamas was furiously trying to pull off the loudspeaker. 'I'm on nights,' he shouted. Really not knowing quite how to stop him, I opened the car door and by accident it hit him where it mattered whereupon he slunk off, speechless and I turned the music off.

ANN HAY (activist)

During the 1964 election, a canvasser said to a woman elector: 'I see someone registered at this address as a Service voter.'

'Yes,' said the lady, 'it's my son who's in the Navy. Put him down as a floating voter.'

And in a council election two years later when my car was covered in stickers for every Conservative candidate in Edinburgh, I was stopped by an elderly bobby for speeding. His opening remark was: 'Aye, lass, you're conservative about everything but your speed.'

MICK LUCKHURST (election aide, Lab)

The old lady was in a wheelchair but we weren't going to let that stop us. It took four men to lift her and her chair into the car, then into the polling station and back into the car. But we did it.

On the way back, she looked at me and said: 'You're all so nice, I feel guilty about voting Conservative.' I thought our driver would have a seizure but, after dropping her (not literally!) I went round to the committee rooms and told the woman there about it. 'I know but I always feel sorry for her,' she said, 'and I was hoping she wouldn't tell you.'

JEREMY HANLEY MP

It was a warm and sunny Tuesday morning during the election campaign of 1983. I had been running through the streets of Barnes, a leafy and attractive part of south west London, stopping to discuss with prospective voters any matters they wanted to raise. Barnes is particularly well populated with members of the acting profession and it's difficult to walk down Barnes High Street without spotting at least two or three famous faces.

On this particular day I was cantering down the road when I was hailed by a pleasant and friendly looking gentleman on the opposite pavement. 'How nice to see you!' he called out, 'I'm going to bed with your mother on Sunday!'

Not every Parliamentary candidate has such an exposé of his mother's private life broadcast to his constituents and further investigation seemed essential. On closer examination the gentleman concerned, who was by now beaming widely no doubt at the thought of his lustful prospects, turned out to be the actor 'Slim' Ramsden, who has appeared in many popular television series and countless plays in the West End of London.

It turned out that both he and my mother, the actress Dinah Sheridan, were appearing together in an edition of the comedy series *Don't Wait up* with Nigel Havers and Tony Britton. The following Sunday they were recording one of the episodes where they ended up in a large double bed. So Mr Ramsden's claim was true and my mother's secret was out! To have one's mother behaving in such a way must have gained me a sympathy vote because the following Thursday I held the seat with a majority of seventy-four and there are at least seventy-four actors in Barnes!

9
Things That Go Bump on the Doorstep

LADY FALKENDER

I was once chased down the street by a man with a lawn mower who clearly had no intention of voting Labour.

ANDREW FOX (activist)

Walking up a long path between the gate and the front door, I spied the householder watering his plants. When I identified my mission, however, he turned the jet of water around and soaked me. I retreated hurriedly – and put him down (on my water-logged canvas card) – as a Wet.

PAMELA HOWARTH (Tory activist)

During the May local elections, a woman voter got almost hysterical about pigeon droppings under a local railway bridge. She thought it was the personal responsibility of Mrs Thatcher.

'No, no,' said the Conservative candidate reassuringly. 'They're definitely Alliance pigeons.'

PAT JOLLY (former agent)

Canvassing in Plymouth I knocked on the door and a little old lady opened it. After I explained my purpose, she said, 'Oh, you're just in time, I have terrible troubles.' Showing the caring concern which would win me her vote, I said: 'Tell me your troubles, maybe I can help.'

'I'm sure you can,' she said, ushering me inside. 'You see, I've gone and lost my glass eye. I just can't find it anywhere.'

There I was, on hands and knees, looking everywhere for the glass eye. Finally, in desperation, I said to her: 'Excuse me but what colour is it?'

She looked at me as if I were a fool: 'It's the same colour as the real one.' Then she paused and said: 'Tell me, what colour *is* it these days?'

ANDREW PEARCE MEP

I suppose that one of the most succinct comments on the election was that of the mongrel dog which crossed the road to urinate on the placard which had my photograph and which I used to advertise my presence. None of the actual voters had the courage to do that.

PAMELA HOWARTH (Tory activist)

While I was out canvassing for the May Council elections, I discovered such a rat-trap of a letter-box that, as well as the leaflet I was distributing, it took hold of my glove.

When I called back later to collect it, I was offered the choice of three gloves . . . so it obviously dealt with all the parties alike!

PETER FOX (activist)

'I've always voted Tory,' she told me eyeing my red rosette. 'And your husband?' 'Oh, he votes the same way I do,' she replied. I smiled: 'Oh, he's henpecked, is he?' I said, just for something to say.

At this, there was a loud bellow from upstairs and I looked up to see probably the most enormous man to exist outside a wrestling ring. He wore a string vest.

'Henpecked? I'll show you henpecked,' and he rushed from the window. The house shook so I assumed he was on his way down and I legged it. My colleague tells me I could sprint for Britain in the Olympics if that man in the string vest were behind me.

'Would that be a maybe or a don't know?'

CATHY LUCKHURST (activist)

The milkman in the village we were canvassing was a mine of statistics and oh, did he like showing off his knowledge. I took the candidate in the house but took the precaution of telling another canvasser, 'Give us ten minutes then come and get us.'

Inside, statistics – about crime, poverty, unemployment, anything – were being reeled round our heads and we kept on looking at our watches. After twenty minutes, not ten, there was finally a knock on the door. 'Take no notice,' said the milkman. 'It's just people wanting milk – I've been up since 4am and they can get their milk from the shop . . . now, as far as abortion is concerned, in 1908 the figures were . . .'

JOHN BROWNE MP

One dark and stormy evening a stalwart Conservative supporter was out canvassing. He came to one garden gate which was unusually difficult to open, being partly tied with string. Undaunted, he succeeded in forcing open the gate and completing what appeared to be a veritable obstacle course (including coils of barbed wire) which appeared to have been laid across the wet and muddy path leading up to the front door. With the aid of a small torch he located the front door bell which he pressed.

He waited and waited. After an interminable delay the house owner switched on the light outside the front door and proceeded to pull back a series of bolts which secured the door itself. The canvasser looked down at his feet to inspect the mud bath in which he believed he was standing, only to find it was concrete. He then realized that he had walked the entire length of a newly laid concrete path leaving deep footprints. The irate house owner finally pulled open the door and with a look of thunder asked, 'What are you doing here?' As quick as a flash the Conservative canvasser said, 'I am canvassing on behalf of the SDP!'

Editor's Note: this 'cement shoes' story also came in from the following:

David Atkinson MP
John Warden, Political Editor, *Daily Express*
Nick Comfort, *Daily Telegraph* Press Gallery
Neil Thorne MP
Keith Speed MP and
Michael Colvin MP
What an astounding coincidence!

10
Yes, But Did You Get the Vote?

DAVID STEEL MP

The incident which I wish to relate took place during the 1966 election. I was in a car cavalcade in Walkerburn, Peeblesshire, and the local Liberals wanted me to get down and meet their oldest resident, a lady of 96. I protested, saying that it would take too much time and I did not want to stop, but they insisted and I finally agreed. I was taken to this old lady who was waiting at the gate with all her family round her. I duly met her and she told me that I was the second MP she had shaken hands with – the first had been Mr Gladstone. As a child of twelve she had presented a bouquet to him during the Midlothian campaign. Needless to say I was bowled over by this and my feelings of annoyance at having my campaign routine interrupted vanished completely.

TREVOR LINDLEY (Bradford)

Some canvassing cards are cryptic. One entry against two names registered at the same address: 'One of these people is dead, didn't wait to find out which.' Was the late occupant in? Did the canvasser arrive dead on time? Above all – whodunnit?

PETER HARDY MP

Early in the last General Election campaign I called on constituents in a small community. The constituent seemed to think it was my fault that they were inundated by peacocks and that the farm nearby had a lot of these decorative nuisances.

I went across to see the farmer. After discussing the weather and the prospects for harvest I mentioned that there seemed to be a lot of peacocks about and he said, 'How many do you think I have?' I had counted twenty-eight and he agreed that was the number. I suggested this was rather a lot and that they would be a nuisance. He agreed but added, 'and it's your fault.'

I was surprised to hear this. I asked him to explain. The farmer said, 'When you came here last to help over the drainage red-tape I mentioned that I was thinking of going into poultry and you remarked that I'd do better with peacocks than with poultry with the present Government in power.'

LORD CLEDWYN OF PENRHOS

A group canvassing for Cledwyn Hughes (as he then was) in an Anglesey village called at a house inhabited by a large family where they knew Cledwyn had been tirelessly helpful over the years. The housewife came to the door and when they asked if she would support Cledwyn she said they hadn't yet decided how they would vote. One of the canvassers thought this a touch circumspect. 'But hasn't he helped you a good deal from time to time?' The housewife looked dubious. 'Maybe, but he hasn't done anything for us recently'.

INIGO BING (activist)

One of my first experiences of canvassing was for Dr David Pitt in Clapham during the 1970 election. I called on a house and asked the lady whether she would be supporting Dr Pitt.

'Oh yes, dear,' she said.

'And your husband?' I asked.

'Oh no dear, he's serving Her Majesty's.'

'Army, Navy or Air Force?'

'No, love, Wandsworth.'

NORMAN ST JOHN STEVAS MP

When I was canvassing at Dagenham, I knocked at a door which was answered by a taciturn gentleman. I asked him whether he was in business. He replied lugubriously that he was. 'Businesses will do better under the Conservatives,' I said. 'What business was it?' 'I'm an undertaker.'

CYRIL SMITH MP

I was canvassing a house when a young girl came to the door. 'Is your Mum in, love?' I enquired. The reply was shattering. 'Flattery will get you nowhere Smith – I am a married woman with two kids.'

BEN PATTERSON MEP

It was raining stairrods, and I was 'knocking up' in a Kent County Council by-election. I trudged up a sodden driveway and rapped on the door. 'Will you be coming out to vote?' I asked the man who opened it. 'Well,' he replied, 'I might.' This was my first success all evening. 'Wonderful,' I said suppressing an inward whoop of delight as I turned and splashed back towards the road.

'And then again,' a voice called after me, 'I might not.'

STAN NEWENS MEP

Just before lunchtime one day during the 1984 European Elections, when I was campaigning in North End Road Market, Fulham, there was an almighty roar of disapproval from behind a stall at something I said and, looking round, I saw a missile hurtling towards me. Putting my hands up quickly to stop it before it landed on my suit, I discovered I had caught a large, ripe tomato in excellent condition.

'Thanks very much,' I boomed into the loudhailer. I ate the tomato with my lunchtime sandwiches. Thoroughly enjoyed it.

LORD JAMES DOUGLAS-HAMILTON MP

I was canvassing very hard in the last election and when a man appeared at one door and I said 'Good morning Sir,' he replied, 'Too late.' 'What?' I asked, 'have the Liberals been here first?' 'No', he said, 'the undertakers took him away last week.' Apart from mentioning my sincere regret I found myself at a loss for words and I hurried on to the next door.

JIM LESTOR MP (Cons)

One of my supporters, out canvassing, came across a bright red front door. Undeterred by such signs of left-wing emulsion, he boldly pressed the bell push, which played 'The Red Flag'. Realizing he may have committed a tactical indiscretion, he was just turning to leave when the door flew open, and a man with a face as red as his political complexion eyed the canvasser's rosette. 'I believe I've got the wrong door', said the canvasser, and shot up the path. (Better red than dead, but better fled than either.)

Portrait of the Artist as a Young Socialist

(Punch, 20 February 1974)

ALAN COREN grows up

I was in a church hall in Reading, once – it can't have been more than, what? Two, three hundred years ago, at the most. I was nineteen – and it was Easter Saturday night. There was nothing significant about Reading, except that that clement spot lies roughly halfway between London and Aldermaston, and the Oxford University Labour Club had rested its caravan there along with fifty thousand other citizens eager to keep the thermonuclear wolf from the door. I lay in a sea of beige duffle, much of it bearded, all of it scarved, thinking. I did a lot of thinking, in those days; there was all this time, you see. You could think for an entire day, doing nothing else, and at the end of it you were still only nineteen. Anyhow, this duffled sea was not entirely calm; indeed, here and there, there were spots of turbulence which gave every known indication that the church hall was in imminent danger of deconsecration, and it was from one such nearby eddy that a girl's voice suddenly said, breathily: 'My God, do you realise that if you were a Conservative, we'd never have met?'

   That's how politics was in those days. An integral part of one's life; there was no point at which life ('For God's sake, try to keep the kids quiet while I try to type this article in order to help pay the back taxes which have mounted to astronomical proportions despite the allowance against them of repayments on a mortgage I could not afford even before its interest rate rose to eleven per cent, while at the same time I calculate whether it is worth selling the furniture to pay for a family holiday, unless the money would be better spent on a decent private room rather than wait for the NHS to determine why it is that every time I cough my vertebrae threaten to fall in a neat pile beside my left shoe, and was that another slate just fell off the roof?') ended, and politics ('Well, I suppose we could always vote Liberal') began, the way there is now. Politics was action (you marched, demonstrated, spoke, wrote), politics was sex (Socialist girls were lush and free, and could kick the door shut from the sofa; Conservative girls were white and reedy and inanimate, and were said to make scones in their spare time), politics was entertainment (drunk on Tunisian claret, you watched the dawn come up in a thousand bedsitters while you speculated noisily on the possibility of edging Hugh Gaitskell down the Trotskyite path, or, logorrhoeic from a surfeit of Wesker or Osborne or some such other turgid prole megaphone at whose feet we would, then, have fallen weeping, you hitch-hiked back up the A40 from London in the small hours, hoping for a lift from a real lorry driver, even a sausage sandwich in a real transport cafe, and therewith the chance to exhort any members of the real working class who would listen to shake off their apathy and, united, lose their chains), politics was, above all, what it was all about, in the days before people learned to say that politics was where it was at.

A note of smugness is already creeping in, I see. In writing about one's own youth, one struggles to avoid both pomposity and sentimentality, and almost inevitably ends up with an uneasy melange of both. Little grates more on the ear, especially the young ear, than the Voice Of Experience; little is more irritating than the balding mortgagee staring at his quarter-acre through his Heal's brandy-balloon and murmuring: 'I used to be quite a rebel in my youth.' Indeed, there are few articles I have wanted less to write, few themes that I would not prefer to pursue; it's just that I feel I ought to write it. This is, after all, a fairly political magazine, it is appearing at a fairly political moment, and a readership has some sort of right to know where its weekly employees stand; or, at any rate, vacillate. No, I lie, it's more than that; for the first time in my life I shall almost certainly be voting Conservative, and if psychiatry has indicated anything, it has indicated that the best way to deal with guilt is to talk about it. A trouble shared is a trouble halved, as Sigmund Freud so succinctly put it.

We shall pause briefly here, to allow members of the congregation to blow raspberries, roll their eyes, marshal the requisite fingers for the due salute, break into *Tell Me The Old, Old Story*, and generally make it known that what is currently defiling the pulpit is a thirty-five-year-old finally emerging in his true colours (a sort of bilious watery blue) and about to claim that his predictable renegation has nothing to do with fears that his already shaky stability will be blown apart by the first gust of red wind that is allowed to penetrate that crack under the bed.

If the row has died down, I have various answers to attempt.

First, it is not treacherous to change one's mind, although, for some reason, it has always been seen as treacherous to change one's *political* mind. If I were to say that, in my youth, I admired Keats or Salinger or Scott Fitzgerald this side of idolatry, and that side, too, but that, a dozen years later, I no longer hold them to be the giants I once thought, no one would call me traitor; nor, if today I revealed that Bach's Toccata and Fugue had shoved Bix Beiderbecke's *Margie* out of my personal Top Ten, would young people come round and throw bricks through my windows in the small hours. *Guernica* is not *The Night Watch*, but I thought it was that and more, once. And surely, if one is permitted to graduate to new literary, or musical, or aesthetic principles, that graduating mind may come to grow towards new political ones without the cries of Judas! and Haw-Haw! following it down the street?

Political theses have to be tested against life, not against other theses. Politics is a life-science, not an academic discipline. This need not mean you will change the views – once, I used to say that *King Lear* was a tragedy rooted in a father's expectation of gratitude, because it looked as though it was; now, I say it is, because I *know* it is – but nor does it mean that you must not, in case the intellect can't cope with the change. It's life that has to do the coping.

Another answer: maturity (all right, age) ripens, along with so much else, cynicism. You come to recognise that idealism is nothing in itself, but that it is a yardstick to check materialism with, and to crack it over the knuckles with, if it threatens to break free and undermine normal human needs and debase them – if it subverts the desire for security, for example, and turns it to greed, if it introduces repression and tries to call it law. Now, that cynicism need not be dignified by calling it, as some do, "healthy cynicism"; it is neither healthy, nor unhealthy, it is scientific, insofar as it is based on evidence which may be objectively checked. You get it from watching the way people are. And while Conservatism lives with that cynicism and accommodates it, Socialism does not. If it tries, it ends up in a Nazi-Soviet pact at worst, it boots out Solzhenitsyn at middling, and, at best, it makes the TUC pretend that what is being done in the name of brotherhood-solidarity has nothing to do with collectivised working-class capitalism, or greed satisfied through the exercise of irresistible power.

The third answer is that Conservatism now is not Conservatism then; which is rather more important than that the Labour Party has likewise changed, because what we were talking about was Socialism as the alternative, not about the Labour Party as the alternative. It was as a Socialist that I rejected the Tories, not as a follower of today's Labour Party, who would, I can tell you, have got short shrift on the

1957 march. What we have now is two contenders claiming to be realistic in their solutions to the island's unease; but one is interlarding its pragmatisms with adipose slabs of the old idealism, which cannot but be seen as the fatty tissues they are.

By the true realist, anyhow.

PETER LEIGHTON (Alliance Candidate in '83 election)

One fine sunny morning midway through the campaign we were canvassing in a quiet road in the west of the constituency and I knocked on the door of a house which was opened by a young Nigerian lady, who was very pleasant and seeking further information about our campaign. Suddenly a small gust of wind caused the door to close behind her and she had no key. Apparently there was a young baby in the house and her husband was abroad on business and would not be returning until the next day. We immediately suggested that we attempt to get in through the back garden but she pointed out that the back door was locked and all the windows were of the louvred type and could not be opened from the outside.

Neighbours gathered and offered help but no-one knew quite how to effect entry to the building without either breaking a window or calling the police or fire brigade – which would hardly be a good advertisement for the Alliance campaign.

After much scratching of heads, it was decided that someone should attempt to enter through the top louvre of the window at the back of the house. The space was, however, extremely narrow and the spectacle of a number of males attempting to squeeze through would clearly do us no credit whatsoever. Finally a very short thin lady agreed to perform the valiant deed. She was supported horizontally by two of my campaign team standing on a ladder and sliding her through the partially open louvred window. When at last she managed to get downstairs and opened the front door the neighbours in the next three houses all took posters and put them in their windows. It's amazing what you can do to garner support for your cause!

PIERS MERCHANT MP

During the December 1985 by-election in the Tyne Bridge constituency, I was canvassing for the Conservative candidate. Tyne Bridge is next door to my own constituency of Newcastle Central and boundary changes obviously cause some confusion. Knocking on one door, I confronted a surprised voter who asked why the election was taking place anyway. I replied, 'Because the sitting Member has unfortunately died.' To which she replied very quickly, and with scarcely concealed delight: 'Oh! I didn't know Piers Merchant had died. Still, I suppose it comes to us all.' I left at once, smiling gravely.

Tony Hall's electoral roles

(Punch, 25 May 1983)

JOHN McWILLIAM MP

'Have you voted yet, love?' asked the Labour canvasser. 'No, I can't leave the baby,' said the young mother. 'I'll hold him for you,' he suggested helpfully. Mother agreed, handed over the baby and promised to return in a flash after voting at the nearby school.

Five minutes passed. Then ten. Then fifteen. Baby's bottom was not as sweet as it once had been, and our canvasser was getting a little behind himself. Twenty minutes later mother returned. 'Sorry,' she chirped, 'but I did a lot of shopping on the way back.'

11
I Wish I'd Said That

ARISTOTLE (384–322 BC)

Man is by nature a political animal.

ROBERT LOUIS STEVENSON (1850–1894)

Politics is perhaps the only profession for which no preparation is thought necessary.

GEORGE BERNARD SHAW (1856–1950)

He knows nothing and he thinks he knows everything. That points clearly to a political career.

WILLIAM SHAKESPEARE (*King Lear*)

Get thee glass eyes
And like a scurvy politician
Seem to see the things thou dost not.

HAROLD MACMILLAN (Lord Stockton)

Sceptical of Harold Wilson's claim that when he was a schoolboy his family had not been able to afford to buy him any boots: 'If Harold Wilson ever went to school without any boots, it was merely because he was too big for them.'

THEODORE ROOSEVELT (1858–1919)

The most successful politician is he who says what everybody is thinking more often and in the loudest voice.

FRANKLIN D. ROOSEVELT (1882–1945)

A radical is a man with both feet planted firmly in the air.

CHARLES FARRAR BROWN (1834–1867)

My pollertics is like my religion, being of an exceedin accomodatin character.

OTTO VON BISMARCK (1815–1898)

Politics is no exact science.

PRESIDENT RONALD REAGAN

I used to say that politics was the second oldest profession and I have come to know that it bears a gross similarity to the first.

FRED DALEY (Australian politician)

Politics is a funny game. One day you're a rooster, the next you're a feather duster.

J. K. GALBRAITH (American economist)

Nothing is so admirable in politics as a short memory.

LORD HAILSHAM

The moment politics becomes dull, democracy is in danger.

LORD TREND (Civil Servant)

As I learnt early on in my life in Whitehall, the acid test of any political question is: What is the alternative?

EUGENE McCARTHY (Presidential candidate)

Being in politics is like being a football coach. You have to be smart enough to understand the game and dumb enough to think it's important.

NIKITA KHRUSCHEV (Russian leader)

Politicians are the same all over. They promise to build a bridge even where there is no river.

MALCOLM MUGGERIDGE

Old politicians, like old actors, revive in the limelight.

PRESIDENT HARRY S. TRUMAN

A politician is a man who understands government and it takes a politician to run a government. A statesman is a politician who's been dead for ten or fifteen years.

THE TIMES

High politics are unsuitable for ordinary men. Great Prime Ministers Winston Churchill and William Pitt were sociable drinkers, Lloyd George and Palmerston could not be trusted with women; Chatham, perhaps greatest of all, was actually mad.

'No, no, you're getting mixed up – the
screaming one wasn't Lord Sutch'

DAVID LLOYD GEORGE (1863–1945)

When introduced at a political meeting with the words: 'I had expected to find Mr Lloyd George a big man in every sense of the word but you see for yourself, he is quite small in stature', Mr Lloyd George replied: 'In North Wales we measure a man from the chin up. You evidently measure from the chin down.'

DAVID LLOYD GEORGE (1863–1945)

A politican is a person with whose policies you do not agree; if you agree with him, he is a statesman.

SIR THOMAS BUXTON (1786–1845)

During the election of 1818 Mr Buxton, Tory candidate for Weymouth, noticed a certain amount of violence from his own supporters towards the opposition. He started his next speech thus:

'Beat them; beat them in the generous exercise of high principles; beat them in disdain of corruption and the display of pure integrity; but do not beat them with bludgeons.'

F. E. SMITH (Lord Birkenhead) (1872–1930)

Having spelt wrongly Lady Wimborne's name, she said: 'How would you like it, Mr Smith, if I misspelt your name?' To which he replied: 'My dear Lady, there is scarcely any alteration you could make which would not add to its distinction.'

At an election meeting, F. E. Smith suggested that a heckler who was constantly interrupting him should take off his cap when asking a question, to which the heckler replied that he would take off his boots if necessary. 'Ah', said Mr Smith, 'I knew you'd come here to be unpleasant.'

SIR WINSTON CHURCHILL (1874–1965)

His comment on developing appendicitis during an election campaign in Dundee in 1922 in which he came bottom of the poll:

'In a twinkling of an eye, I found myself without office, without a seat, without a party and without an appendix.'

'Would you like to tell our readers, sir,' a journalist asked Churchill, 'what are the desirable qualifications for any young man who wishes to be a politician?' Churchill put on his bulldog look. 'It is the ability to foretell what is going to happen tomorrow, next week, next month and next year. (Pause) And to have the ability afterwards to explain why it didn't happen.'

Churchill on the stump describing his opponent Clement Atlee: 'Atlee is a sheep in sheep's clothing.'

And: 'Mr Atlee is a very modest man. But then, he has much to be modest about.'

HILAIRE BELLOC (1870–1953)

On standing for the first time for Parliament as a Liberal in South Salford and being a Roman Catholic, he was advised by the Church that his religion would not help him, that he'd best be quiet about it. He retorted by opening his first speech in this way:

'I am a Catholic. As far as possible, I go to Mass every day. This is a rosary (taking it from his pocket) – as far as possible I kneel down and tell these beads every day. If you reject me on account of my religion, I shall thank God that he has spared me the indignity of being your representative.'

LORD JOHN GRETTON

At the General Election of 1935, Lord Gretton's Socialist opponent was a Mrs G. Paling. At one of her meetings, Mrs Paling shouted: 'John Gretton is a dirty dog.' A Gretton supporter in the audience shouted back: 'That's as may be but we all know what dirty dogs do to palings.'

LADY ASTOR

A heckler during a political meeting: 'Say Missus, how many toes are there on a pig's foot?' Lady Astor: 'Take off your boots, man, and count for yourself.'

One of Lady Astor's main opponents in the Labour Party was W. T. Gay, a man of pacifist tendencies. She responded: 'Mr Gay represents the shirking classes, I represent the working classes. If you can't get a fighting man, get a fighting woman.'

Or you may prefer this one: 'Something awfully funny happened to me in London the other day. I saw a young American sailor outside the House of Commons and said to him: "Would you like to go in?" He said: "You're the sort of woman my mother warned me against." '

LORD JACOBSON

This is reported to be a true story. It occurred at a meeting supporting Joe Reeves MP in the years between the wars when local meetings were rather better attended than they are today.

A crowded meeting was in progress and was being addressed by the candidate. In the front seat there was a drunken man who at every pause in the candidate's speech said: 'You bloody fool.' Eventually the speaker said: 'Take no notice of that man. He is drunk.' Immediately the man responded, plagiarizing Winston Churchill slightly, 'Yes, but I'll be sober in the morning and you will still be a bloody fool.'

PRESIDENT LYNDON JOHNSON

On being introduced in over-flattering terms: 'I do so wish that my parents could have been present today. My father would have liked what was said about me. My mother would have believed it.'

12
I Wish I Hadn't Said That

SIR ALASTAIR BURNET

One night on *News at Ten* a report came through that a county council in south-west England was thinking of restoring corporal punishment in schools. Through some aberration I said on air the council was thinking of restoring 'capital punishment'.

Many viewers kindly rang to ask if I had had a small refreshment before giving tongue to this. I had had no idea that I'd said any such thing, but was eventually persuaded I had by a friendly letter from a viewer saying he thought capital punishment in schools an excellent, if novel, concept and, as he had several of his own children in mind, could I let him have the names of any good schools in the south-west.

IAIN DALE (PA to Patrick Thompson MP)

I was campaigning on a relatively well-to-do housing estate, knocked on the door and went into the usual spiel of asking for the voter's support. His reply was: 'I've half a mind to vote SDP.'

My instant, ill-considered reply was: 'Well, half a mind is all you need really,' before the door was slammed in my face.

NICK COMFORT (*Daily Telegraph* Press Gallery)

A friend was canvassing for the Labour Party and was sent to a small owner-occupied estate in an Essex town largely peopled by present and former RAF officers. At one door, a man with a magnificent moustache emerged, asked him his business and when told, replied: 'I'm, terribly sorry old boy, I always vote Conservative!' To which my friend replied: 'You shouldn't be sorry, you should be **** ashamed of yourself.'

DR MARK HUGHES MP

The candidate and his agent were doing an afternoon canvass of a narrow street, one on either side of the road.

The candidate could hear over his shoulder that the agent was getting flack from the woman opposite so he turned and called tactfully: 'Gerry, can you come and help with this one please?' Gerry peeled himself away from his noisy doorstep and came stomping up the path in disgust, muttering, 'That silly old bag has lost her marbles.' We heard a snort, and our heads swivelled towards the voter on the doorstep. 'That "silly old bag" is my mother!'

ANDREW PEARCE MEP

I have only once been suspected of megalomania, and this was due entirely to a technical fault on our radio car's public address system. My voice had been broadcast all day saying 'This is Andrew Pearce your Conservative candidate. Support the Conservative Government.' Unfortunately, when the gremlin got into the works, the message came blaring out, 'This is Andrew Pearce your Conservative Government'.

Me and My Junta
(Punch, 9 October 1974)

Want an idle, benevolent, pleasure-seeking Dictator?
You couldn't do better than AUBERON WAUGH

Nothing but the most acute discomfort in the personal circumstances of my life would ever persuade me to assume power, and my purpose in doing so would be not so much to restructure society as to remove myself from those elements in it which were causing me distress. This is the invariable advice I give to those who, for one reason or another, wish to restructure society. No good ever comes of trying to impose one's wishes on other people. The great thing is to avoid unpleasantness. The assumption of supreme power may seem an extreme way to set about this, and is certainly not something to be undertaken until all other remedies have failed.

Since my purpose in assuming power is simply to retire to a little court of beautiful, clever, kind and funny people, my main objective, when in power, would be to consolidate my position. This new Versailles might be set up in Hampton Court Palace, but more likely in my present roomy abode in West Somerset where you meet a better class of person, generally speaking, than in the London area. We need not concern ourselves here with the mechanics of assuming power. I imagine it involves no more than informing as many people as possible that you have assumed it. If one persistently makes oneself disagreeable enough to enough people, one can usually get one's way in this country. Serious opponents will have to be overcome by pretending to agree with them wholeheartedly, asking them to lunch and poisoning them. As I say, the assumption of power is not something to be undertaken except under extreme provocation.

The consolidation of this power might be more difficult. There is no point in assuming power for a few years and then ending upside down on a petrol pump. I expect at very least to found a dynasty, and my eldest son is still only ten, although making good progress in maths, French and the violin. Since nobody can govern in Britain nowadays without the consent of the working class, the only way round is to recognize the power of organized labour and contain it within a Constitution. Organized labour would constitute a second Chamber with powers of delay or, ultimately, veto on any domestic proposals I might make. This need not worry me in the least as I do not intend to make any. In exchange for this position of enormous privilege and power as the centre of Government, organised labour will be required to make two concessions: (1) power workers and key workers in certain industries should 'sell' their right to strike as in France, in exchange for a fixed and absurdly high multiple of the average national wage; (2) strikers would only be permitted to picket their own place of work, and nobody who did not work there would be permitted to picket it. Army and police would be kept fanatically loyal by presents of whisky, opium and Mars Bars.

There would be no need for me to take any steps to solve our balance of payments crisis since the logic of the situation demands it must solve itself. After Arab oil is exhausted and North Sea oil has replaced it, and after we have repudiated the Middle Eastern currency mountain and nationalised Arab investments in this country, it follows as night follows day that international payments will have to be settled in gold, around which every currency (including the dollar, but probably not the Eurodollar which will have been repudiated, too) can float to its heart's content. I might ask Peter Jay to decide how much money

I WISH I HADN'T SAID THAT

111

should be printed from time to time (if he would like to join my Junta) as he seems to be interested in this sort of thing, but I can't believe it makes much difference. Perhaps I could persuade him to print rather less before my summer holidays every years so that I will get a reasonable rate of exchange in French restaurants.

For the most part, then, I would be a rather low-profile dictator. Freedom of speech would be absolute except in times of war, when nobody would be allowed to insult the Dictator. In times of peace, a large part of the Dictator's role would be as a sort of national Aunt Sally, a symbol on which its citizens could vent their frustration and a release for all the energies which they at present waste on complaining about their old age pensions. I would spend nearly all my time in my palace at Combe Florey, dancing reels, dallying with ladies-in-waiting, eating, drinking and listening to the best things our civilisation has to offer in the way of food, wine and music, and making satirical jokes about the day's news when in the mood. Occasionally, I should emerge on the nation's television sets to make important pronouncements on burning issues of the day – football, hooliganism or new developments in the war with Sweden. My material for these pronouncements would come from the morning's leading article in *The Times*, which few people ever read.

Oh yes, I had forgotten to mention my war with Sweden. This would be my first and only foreign policy initiative, to declare war on Sweden within a few days of coming to power. It would be planned to last a hundred years, just like the Hundred Years War, with occasional breaks for refreshment, and would be the most boring war in history, with no causes, no consequences, no heroic action and no great national leaders. In fact, nobody would ever do anything about the war, except hurl abuse and blood-curdling threats at the other side over the wireless. No troops would ever leave our shores for Sweden, and it seems most unlikely that the Swedes would attempt what Napoleon and Hitler failed to do and invade England. Citizens of the two belligerent countries who met each other on neutral ground would pointedly look the other way, and from time to time I would appear on television and announce I was seriously thinking of resorting to germ warfare, or using the ultimate deterrent.

My reason for this exercise would be partly that I have always found Swedes – with only one exception – the most tiresome people; partly that they are a smaller nation than we are and also rather unaggressive and so would probably fall in with my schemes – I would never try this policy on the Irish, for instance. But most of all it is to instil the spirit of national unity and self-sacrifice which only comes about, for some reason, in wartime, and which is so essential to our country in its present dilemma. Nobody would complain, everybody would set about his daily task, be it never so humble, with the dogged determination to win through which has made Britain what it is.

From time to time, as I have said, I would declare a truce, in the course of which everyone would be free to insult me. As soon as anyone said anything really wounding, however – like I was getting too fat – I would blow my whistle and announce that the war had started up again.

There, then, would be the general pattern of my rule. Of course, things like law and order would have to go on. If violent crime got out of hand I would equip a remote island in the Outer Hebrides with concrete bunkers, and condemn violent criminals to live there for the rest of their lives. They would be completely unsurveyed, free to murder each other or commit any atrocities against each other that they liked. The only surveillance would be from a coastguard station on a neighbouring island, to make sure that nobody ever escaped, but nobody would ever land there, except heavily armed detachments of marines to drop new prisoners. There would be no medical attention, no chaplain (unless some doctor or clergyman happened to be a prisoner), none of the comforts of civilisation unless they improvised them and no contact with the outside would except at Christmas, when a helicopter would drop plum puddings on them from a great height, the gift of some charitable foundation.

No doubt there are many things which need to be done to improve Britain. When I was young and foolish I used to play with all sorts of radical ideas, like abolishing the public schools, declaring progeniture illegal, getting the unemployed to pull down unsightly modern buildings, forbidding the use of transistor wirelesses in public, abolishing private property, imposing a large tax on budgerigars. My sad conclusion, in maturity, is any attempt to improve things for people usually ends by making it worse. If people can't improve things for themselves, they must just learn to live in an imperfect world.

As I say, I hope it will never come to this. The only precaution I have taken is to lay in large supplies of Paraquat which I earnestly hope I shall never have to use. Nowadays whenever I shut the great gates of my gatehouse, I have the illusion that I am already the Dictator of Britain I described. Just as long as nobody does anything to disturb that happy illusion.

BILL BOOTH (activist)

As a candidate in the 1983 General Election, I came across an 80-year-old Derbyshireman in the garden. After I introduced myself he said 'Alliance!' in tones of complete scorn. 'Ah,' I said, 'there's a lot less difference between David Steel and David Owen than there is, for example, between Ted Heath and Maggie Thatcher.' 'Happen,' said the man shaking his head, 'but I tell you, two cocks in one pen nivver did agree.'

PATRICK CORMACK MP

My first successful General Election campaign was in the glorious June of 1970. Standing in the back of a Land Rover two days before polling day I felt surprisingly relaxed, in spite of all the dire predictions of the polls, as we bumped our way down a very narrow country lane heading for one of the smallest villages in the constituency. I could just see above the deep banked hedgerows into the field where cows were munching contentedly. In playful mood I chattered into the loudspeaker, 'Now, come on, you old cows – I can do with your support!' Suddenly we rounded a corner and my face fell. Emerging from a Women's Institute meeting, a phalanx of jam-makers stood transfixed, staring at the radio car with something less than electoral fervour.

BOB PARSONS (activist)

A canvasser – not me! – once suggested to a Tory supporter on his doorstep that his party's policies were 'a load of balls'. The voter replied that he would not vote Labour if they had such rude members.

As the canvasser walked away, his mood changed by degrees from towering triumph to detachment, from detachment to chagrin, and from chagrin to downright anxiety. He later returned to the same house to say that he had actually meant *golf* balls.

VIC TURTON (former Lord Mayor of Birmingham and Labour County Councillor)

A teenage, dead-keen new canvasser was sent with me so he could pick up Labour techniques to bring in the vote. We went to a block of flats and after a while, I decided he could be trusted to go to one flat on his own while I went to the one next door. As I came out after canvassing my flat, I heard a commotion coming from the neighbouring one. My young canvasser came running out, followed by shouts of 'F--- off, we're all Labour here!'

TIM RENTON MP

I was canvassing in Sheffield during a hot June evening and found myself looking through the open window at a burly steel worker who was soaking himself in the bath. Embarrassed, I looked at his garden and saw it was full of primroses.

'Did you know that primroses were Disraeli's favourite flowers?' I asked.

'Is that so?' he replied, 'In that case I'll dig the buggers up tomorrow.'

TONY SPELLAR MP

An MP, referring to one of his opponents in a General Election famous for his gaffes: 'Here is one who only opens his mouth to change feet.'

COUNCILLOR KEITH DIBBLE

At about 6.30pm on election day, the enemy Conservative loud-speaker car turned into an apparently deserted street but one which housed, as luck would have it, a crowded fish and chip shop.

'You know,' observed the loudspeaker suddenly (its handler rashly having a little chat with his driver without switching off the machine). 'Aldershot must be the most ghastly town I've ever been to.'

As the Conservatives came bottom of the poll, it seems that from that day forward they'd had their chips.

HENRY BELLINGHAM MP

During the midst of a heated 1983 General Election campaign, I knocked on the door of a flat to be greeted by a 30-year-old Jehovah's Witness. He was broad Norfolk so it was not easy following what he said, but the gist of it was that he thought all politicans were equally objectionable. Halfway through our increasingly friendly conversation a very frail, elderly lady appeared, said hello and tottered back into her bedroom.

Thinking I might clinch the vote with a few kind words on departure, I called, 'Say goodbye to your mother for me – or is it your grandmother?'

The rejoinder was as swift as it was unintelligible. 'Eer, ger yor ought moi flat, that's *moi woif*.'

'*Mr Bloggs therefore forfeits his deposit*'

NICHOLAS FAIRBAIRN MP

In the February 1974 election, the tide was running strongly in favour of the Scottish Nationalist Party. The local Tories were in a state of panic.

In Auchterarder I met the chairman and secretary of the local Association before going canvassing. They warned me that 'All the old ladies are going SNP.' I was asked to walk down the street and charm them, keeping a particular eye open for one prominent lady who had fingers in every local pie.

In due course, I came across the lady in sensible tweeds and brogues. 'Good morning,' I said charmingly, adding: 'I hear you're voting for those f***ing Nationalists.' My majority, excluding her, was 53.

SIR ANTONY BUCK MP

I am always amazed at the courtesy which usually greets one when one is canvassing, but there is the occasional exception.

Once, I was accosted at the door by a lady who, on seeing my large rosette and perhaps recognizing me, gave forth a string of vitriolic and very unparliamentary expletives, to which, with a name like Buck, I can be vulnerable. Wishing to avoid a scene that might besmirch the neighbourhood, I backed down the path, a little disconcerted, and bowing deeply, said, 'Madam, you are quite the most enchanting virago I have met with in years,' hoping this would smooth my path back to the gate. Her face lit up like a firecracker. 'And don't use that filthy language to me,' she bellowed, 'or I'll set the police on you!'

13
Canvassing a Laugh

ANONYMOUS MP

A senior Tory politician was at his desk when his secretary said the Prime Minister was on the phone. All the secretary heard from him was, 'No, no, no, yes, no. Goodbye.'

'Well, you certainly told her,' said the secretary, 'but what was the "Yes"?'

'Oh,' he said, 'she just asked me if I was still listening.'

MALCOLM RIFKIND MP

A definition of a diplomat is one who is disarming even if his country isn't!

A. CECIL WALKER MP

During a hectic electioneering campaign, two slightly jaded Tory MPs were discussing the mundane aspects of their present existence.

'How's your sex life these days?' says one.

'Infrequently,' replied the other.

'Is that one word or two?'

GREG KNIGHT MP

I like the story about the MP, away at a conference, who met a nubile young lady in the hotel foyer. A few drinks led to another and then they signed in the register as Mr and Mrs Smith and went upstairs for an enjoyable night.

The next day, the MP was presented with a bill for £500. 'Look here,' he told the manager, 'I have only stayed here one night.'

'Yes sir,' said the manager, 'but your wife has been here for six weeks.'

SYDNEY CHAPMAN MP

I was the only architect in the House when I lost my seat in 1974. I concluded my speech to my supporters by saying I was the only unsuccessful politician who could say literally, 'Ah well, back to the drawing board.'

NICHOLAS WINTERTON MP

When Winston Churchill had a meeting with his counterpart, the Prime Minister of Ireland, both countries were facing serious problems. Churchill commented that, in his view, the situation in the UK was serious but not hopeless. The Irish PM replied that the situation in his country was hopeless but not serious.

SIR EDWARD DU CANN MP

The trouble with political jokers is that some of them get elected.

ANGELA RUMBOLD MP

During the course of the by-election, my daughter and I were wearing shirts with 'I'm not perfect but parts of me are excellent' written on the front – I can't remember why.

On the whole, women voters were dubious, whereas the men tended to take it all in good part.

JOE ASHTON MP

It is a very tense debate in the House of Commons and Willie Hamilton is accusing Harold Wilson of ratting on his committment to the Common Market.

'First he is for the Market,' thunders Willie. 'Then he is against. This is not the politics of leadership . . . it is the politics of *coitus interruptus*.'

There is a shocked silence then an indignant voice yells: 'Withdraw.'

LORD MURRAY (formerly Len Murray of the TUC)

'Leave nothing to chance' was the slogan of the candidate for Mayor of Tombstone, Arizona. He had left no hand unshaken, no offspring's head unpatted, either of any voter in, or any bemused casual visitor to, Tombstone. At his eve-of-poll meeting, in the town's main saloon – where else – he came to the peroration of his address. 'That's what I stand for,' he said. 'That's what I believe in for this town and always have. Them's my standards, my principles. And if you don't like 'em, I'll change 'em.'

'The moderates, I feel, would be
prepared to keep their unreasonable
demands within limits'

TERRY DAVIS MP

Four people were arguing about who had the oldest profession in the world.

'Mine is the oldest profession in the world,' said the Lawyer. 'If you look in the Bible, you will see that Cain killed Abel and got away with it. Obviously, he must have been defended by someone, and that is the job of a Lawyer so I represent the oldest profession in the world.'

'Not so,' said the Doctor. 'If you look further back in the Bible, you will see how God used Adam's rib to create Eve. Someone must have healed Adam's side. That is the job of a Doctor, so I represent the oldest profession in the world.'

'No, no,' said the Architect. 'Go right back to the beginning of the Bible, and you will see that God created the world by bringing order out of chaos. When you think about it, the job of the Architect is to bring order out of chaos, and it follows that I represent the oldest profession in the world.'

Last to speak was the Prime Minister. 'No gentlemen, you are all wrong,' she said. 'Mine is the oldest profession in the world. *After all, who created the chaos?'*

A. CECIL WALKER MP

Politics is like a race horse. A good jockey must know how to fall with the least possible damage.

An election year is the year in which it *will* be necessary to fool all of the people all of the time.

It is amazing to see how a minority, reaching a majority, seizing authority, rates a minority.

Overheard at a selection meeting: 'What do you think of our two candidates?'

'Well, I'm glad only one can be elected.'

A candidate came home in the small hours and gave his wife the glorious news. 'Darling, I have been elected.' She was delighted. 'Honestly?' she said. He laughed in an embarrassed way. 'Oh, why bring that up?'

I wonder if those who assert there isn't a perfect man in the world have ever heard an election campaign speech?

Fainting on the Way

(Punch, 25 September 1974)

WILLIAM DAVIS

But the country has too much reason to know the difference between promise and performance . . .

That, as you will have recognised at once, is a quotation from the Liberal Party's 1922 Election Manifesto. No, I promise you, they really said it. Labour, that year, proposed 'a system of taxation which will distribute the burden fairly according to ability to pay,' and the Tories maintained that 'at home our chief preoccupation at this time is the state of trade and employment.'

Old manifestoes have long been among my favourite reading at Election time, if only because they serve as a reminder that crises are nothing new and that economic problems have dominated British politics for more years than anyone cares to remember. Throughout we have had appeals to national unity, as in the coalition manifesto of 1918:

Well and truly have rich and poor, castle and cottage, stood the ordeal of fire. Right earnestly do we trust that the united temper, the quiet fortitude, the high and resolute patriotism of our nation may be long preserved into the golden times of peace.

They don't make rhetoric like that any more, though it isn't for want of trying. Some of the other issues of 1918 seem just as familiar:

Ireland is unhappily rent by contending forces . . .

And of course

It will be the duty of the new Government to remove all existing inequalities of the law as between men and women.

One recurring theme which no longer appears in manifestoes was the 'excessive consumption of alcoholic drink'. According to the Liberals' 1923 Manifesto it was

One of the main causes of unemployment, disease and poverty.

Labour's *Appeal to the People* in 1924 contained references to other topics which sound odd today. It promised, for example, a bill to prevent Frauds in the Sale of Bread, and proposals 'to prevent the still existing evils of Sweating'.

Then, as now, however

The path to our goal is long and narrow and sometimes so hard to travel that men and women faint on the way.

Seven years later those who hadn't fainted were told by a National Government that

Some of the problems that lie before us are wide as the world itself: some are peculiar to ourselves.

The Conservative leader insisted that

We must shrink from no steps to prove the stability of our country and to save our people from the disaster attaching to our currency fluctuating and falling through lack of confidence at home and abroad.

While Labour's Ramsay McDonald was adamant that

WE MUST ALL PULL TOGETHER

An election, he said, was necessary 'to demonstrate to the whole world the determination of the British people to stand by each other in times of national difficulty and to support any measure required for placing themselves and their credit in an unassailable position.'

The Liberals agreed that this was

NO TIME FOR HAGGLING

In 1935 the three leaders of the National Government published a joint manifesto, but the Labour Opposition claimed that

The Government has conducted a campaign of fraud, misrepresentation, and panic . . . it is plunging the nation into an electoral struggle in the midst of an international crisis.

In the first election campaign after the war Churchill was back to the need for unity

Upon our power to retain unity, the future of this country and of the whole world largely depends.

But Labour thought that

in themselves they are no more than words . . . it is very easy to set out a list of aims . . . what matters is whether it is backed up by a genuine workmanlike plan conceived without regard to sectional vested interest and carried through in a spirit of resolute concentration.

And of course

The future will not be easy.

Five years later the Conservative manifesto insisted that

The Labour Government have shrunk from the realities of the situation and have not told the people the truth.

While Labour, heading its manifesto *Let us Win Through Together*, asked for

Continued, mighty efforts from us all

And the Liberals argued that

Crisis after crisis comes upon us, because we are living beyond our means.

I won't go on. What all this shows, clearly, is that history *does* repeat itself, and that political platitudes have a remarkably long life. The irony is, of course, that throughout these years of crisis the vast majority of Britons have become more and more affluent; there is no comparison between 1918 and 1974.

Manifestoes *have* become longer over the years (inflation leaves nothing untouched) and one can't help wondering who actually reads them. It is stretching the imagination a bit far to picture the housewife in Sheffield poring over the offerings while she does the ironing, or the bus driver in Stepney devoting his lunch break to a careful study of Keith Joseph's views on the money supply. Millions of people merely vote the way they have always done; arguments are wasted on them. But even the serious student of politics, making a brave attempt to plough through the acres of print after work or at the weekend, would find it hard to digest all that verbiage between now and October 10.

I dare say many people have a go. But they may well end up more, rather than less, confused. The trouble with party programmes is that you can't pick out the bits you like and ignore the rest: you have to swallow the lot. So if you are anti-Common Market, but intensely dislike the idea of nationalisation, you have to weigh up whether the first bit outweighs the second sufficiently to make you vote Labour. Ditto if you think Labour has the right approach to inflation but regard Harold Wilson as a disastrous leader.

The Tories seem to set much store by a single promise – Mrs. Thatcher's 9½ percent mortgages – and it may well be that, despite all that has been said about the latest economic crisis, people will still fall for such a simple and obvious ploy. Or it may be the colour of Mr. Heath's tie on October 10th; *he* may want to keep personalities out of politics this time but the press and TV (let alone Labour and Liberal candidates) are unlikely to give him that satisfaction.

The people who really have my sympathy are those who, in the end, will have to try to make all these ambitious programmes work. It is one thing for politicians and their backroom boys to think up tax revolutions (every party is determined to undo everything introduced by its rivals) and to devise impressive-sounding schemes for everything from the control of incomes to 'a wide-ranging programme of social reform'. It is, alas, quite another to administer them fairly and efficiently.

Many people in Whitehall – especially in the Inland Revenue – feel that politics has lost contact with reality. The feeling is shared in industry, which has to plan years ahead and needs at least some assurance of stability. There are too *many* policies, not too few. The never-ending search for instant miracle cures, for schemes which sound appealing and are sufficiently different to win votes, has created a background of confusion which makes economic problems worse rather than better. Some companies are currently in trouble because Mr. Heath changed strategy at a stroke, and because Mr.

Wilson has charged off in yet another direction. Others have postponed plans to build new plant (and therefore create employment) until they see whether Britain means to stay in Europe or not. Uncertainty is *always* bad for business.

Bookmakers, we are told, are betting on another stalemate – with, presumably, the prospect of yet another election in 1974 unless there is a coalition. Academics like Professor Finer seem to think we should welcome such an outcome; he must be joking.

JOHN SMITH (Features Editor, *Sunday People*)

A Tory politician told a rally: 'I was born an Englishman, I have lived all my life as an Englishman, and I hope to die an Englishman.'

'What's wrong?' said an Irish voice from the back. 'Have you no ambition?'

A hostile voter once accosted Winston Churchill after an election in which Winston had retained his seat. The voter said with a sneer: 'I presume we may expect you to continue to be humbly subservient to the powerful interests that control your vote?'

With a growl, Churchill replied: 'I'll thank you to keep my wife's name out of this.'

Voter: 'I don't belong to any organized political party.'
Canvasser: 'In that case, I'll put you down as SDP.'

A Labour candidate was addressing a group of Fleet Street print workers and told them confidently: 'I guarantee that if you elect a Labour government you will all be working a four day week.'

'Stuff that,' said one printer. 'I'm not working an extra two days a week for anyone.'

The political meeting lapsed into uproar when one of the audience stood up and shouted: 'Mrs Thatcher has a face like a sheep's backside.'

'How dare you,' retorted a man in the middle of the crowd. 'I have never heard anything so insulting in my life.'

'Are you a Tory supporter?' inquired the candidate.

'No,' said the man. 'I'm a shepherd.'

Walking alone along a river bank one day, Mrs Thatcher slipped and fell into the fast-flowing water. A 14-year-old boy heard her cries for help, plunged in and pulled her out.

'How can I repay you?' asked the Prime Minister. 'You can have anything – just name it.'

'I'd like a state funeral,' replied the lad.

'A state funeral?' echoed Mrs Thatcher. 'But you're still only a boy.'

'I know,' said the youngster. 'But my Dad's been on the dole for two years and when I tell him who I pulled out of the river he'll kill me.'

ROBERT ATKINS MP

The defeated candidate walking down the street the morning of the election, had a great grin on his face. When asked why, he said: 'If you'd heard the election promises I made, *you'd* be glad you lost.'

GREG KNIGHT MP

An ardent feminist was addressing some of her colleagues on the evils of smoking. 'I have been an MP for five years,' she said, 'and have never put a cigarette between my lips.' To which an old boy responded: 'Madam, I have been an MP for twenty-five years and have never put one anywhere else.'

NORMAN ST JOHN STEVAS MP

I had an amusing experience with a child at Chelmsford, during the last election when I asked him how old he was. He replied, 'Seven – how old are you?' At that I changed the subject and asked him where he went to school. The answer came 'I go to a Catholic School but my sister goes to a Christian one.' I replied, 'That is a distinction without a difference,' and fled!

ANONYMOUS MP

The President of the United States said to his friends, the President of France and the Prime Minister of Britain: 'I have a terrible problem, I have eighteen bodyguards and one is a member of the KGB and I cannot find out which one it is.'

The President of France retorted: 'That's nothing, I have eighteen mistresses and one is unfaithful to me and I cannot find out which one it is.'

'My dilemma is worst of all,' said the Prime Minister of Britain. 'I have eighteen people in my Cabinet and one of them is quite clever . . . and I cannot find out which one it is.'

THE VISCOUNT ST DAVIDS

There had been a by-election in one of the great deserted areas of North Scotland and a London evening paper was commenting on the new MP. But there was a crisis at the paper and some severe sub-editing had been done to the story. It finally appeared with the comment: 'The new member wears a kilt. It takes him six weeks to cover his huge constituency.'

SIR ELDON GRIFFITHS MP

1. Extracts from the Metropolitan Police Disciplinary book of 1886 are said to include the following:

   (i) Constable Abercrombie – dismissed from the force. Charge: going around knocking on doors, asking for a drink of water, in the hope of getting beer or spirits – and far too often succeeding!

   (ii) Sergeant Blenkinsop – reduced to constable. Charge: discovered while on duty, off his beat, in bed with a married woman, not his wife, with his boots on!

2. Asked to investigate why a certain Brigadier in a rural village had failed to obtain a shotgun licence, the village PC discovered that the old soldier not only had no shotgun licence but had also been using an elephant gun.

   The PC's report read as follows:

   'For the past fifteen years, I have diligently patrolled this village, the copses and woods around, and never once have I encountered an elephant. This goes to show that the Brigadier has been doing a first class job. I therefore recommend that he keep his shotgun, lest an elephant should stray into this village from a less well patrolled part of Suffolk.'

FRED CHAPMAN (Councillor)

A Socialist's Prayer:

Grant me, O Lord, the genius to explain to my comrades, the rules and constitution of our Great Party. Even though no one explains them to me.

Give to me the intelligence, the wisdom and the knowledge to understand them that I may evaluate their impact on my Comrades. Even though no one shows me how to evaluate them, and no one is quite sure if they are, in fact, of any value at all.

Give to me the understanding that I may forgive the apathetic, curb the over-ambitious, and accept the views of the comrade who does nothing until I have done something and then tells me how I should have done it, and what I should have done.

Make me formidable in debate, logical in argument, fearless in confrontation – Lawyer, Actor, Philosopher, Sociologist and Economist – pleading, cajoling, threatening, belabouring so that I may make the best from a good case, and a good case from no case at all.

Teach me, O Lord, to stand with both feet firmly on the ground, even though I haven't a leg to stand on.

O Lord, let my comrades see the future as a great Commonwealth of all persons, and, when they at last believe in it – give me the physical strength to stop the punch ups that ensue.

Lord, I am Chairman of the Birmingham Labour Party, I pray that you, in your infinite wisdom, see my need for all these things, and, in your great mercy, grant them to me.

                                                              Amen.

*'I believe we've got a winner, Jeffrey –
he's started healing people!'*

JOHN HOWARD CORDLE (former MP)

A useful Grace for formal and informal occasions:

'Prevent us, O Lord, from being stodgy and hard to stir like porridge. Please make us more like cornflakes, "ready to serve".'

14
An Inside View

NORMAN WILLIS (General Secretary, TUC)

I work hard, then sleep like a baby. Yes, just like a baby. Sleep an hour . . . cry an hour . . . sleep an hour . . . cry an hour . . .

JOHN WAKEHAM MP

After some years as Chief Whip, I have discovered that those who know most about politics are too busy either cutting hair or driving taxis to do anything about it.

AUSTIN MITCHELL MP

I was showing a party of constituents around the House of Commons and as I stood there explaining what the Central Lobby was all about, Neil Kinnock and one of his aides walked across it. Another Labour MP saw him and shouted, to stop him: 'Neil! Neil!'

At that, my party all dropped to their knees and Neil Kinnock laughed: 'No, come on, that's not necessary. Well, not yet anyway.'

CHARLES KENNEDY MP

As the SDP candidate on the Monday of election week, I rolled onto the Skye ferry in the campaign car which was covered in 'Kennedy X' posters. A local came up in a great state of excitement, pointing at the car and saying, 'Where is he? Where is he? I've always wanted to meet him!' When informed that I was 'he', the local looked crestfallen and muttered something about always having been a great fan of the well-known Gaelic singer Calum Kennedy.

Then there was the time I arrived early in a dinner jacket for a charity thrash and was directed down the corridor to the first door on the left. Assuming this would be free snout-in-the-trough-time-for-VIPs, I was puzzled to discover a rather bare room with heaps of empty boxes. Not being musical it hadn't occurred to me that the doorman assumed me to be the lead singer with the band.

But the biscuit for ego-deflation goes to the little girl from the constituency who participated in a primary school visit to Westminster. Afterwards, I duly signed the Tour Guide for each pupil and when I handed back the last one, the little girl looked at me with a wide-eyed, captivating stare. I succumbed on the spot. 'Is there anything else dear?'

'Oh yes please, Mr Kennedy, can you do me a big favour?'

'Of course,' said I, driving further into Mugsville. 'Just name it.'

'Well,' said the little girl, 'could you please get me Neil Kinnock's autograph?'

LLOYD TURNER (Editor, *Daily Star*)

Perhaps you might not have heard the tale of Eric Moonman knocking on a constituency door and announcing: 'Good morning, I'm canvassing on behalf of Moonman . . .' And being told by the bellicose voter: 'Moonman? It's time you buggers came down to earth!'

And then there are the stories of those whose progress to Westminster has been impeded by their unfortunate names, like the Hon. Member for Falmouth and Cambourne who has to find ways of introducing himself other than: 'Good morning, my name is Mudd.' Percy Grieve, QC, succeeded in becoming the Tory Member for Solihull despite a campaign which resulted in his constituency being plastered with posters which ambiguously declaimed 'GRIEVE FOR SOLIHULL.' Sir Bernard Braine's poster campaign in Essex South-East also hit snags: it seemed to him that graffiti artists had managed to deface every single poster by adding the prefix 'BIRD' to his name.

While our own award-winning columnist Joe Ashton tells of a predecessor in his constituency called Dyer, whose worthy addresses on the hustings were constantly interrupted by urchins calling: 'We don't want Dyer 'ere in Bassetlaw' (Say it out loud to get the full flavour of this witticism!).

Joe also tells me the perfectly true story of his appearance in a Labour Party political broadcast before the last General Election. Apparently these films are made in a rather grotty little studio in Wardour Street, right in the heart of Soho, and Joe was having trouble finding the right place. At that time, he was too proud or vain to admit that he needed glasses, and was peering short-sightedly at name-plates and postcards which read simply 'Rosie', 'Desiree', 'French model', 'Large chest for sale' and the like, when he was approached by a London bobby.

'Good morning, Mr Ashton,' said the constable. 'Can I help you?'

'You're not going to believe this,' said Joe, with the despairing feeling that his forecast was absolutely right, 'but I'm making a party political broadcast . . .'

The officer's sceptical expression made it plain to Joe that he preferred to believe he had caught yet another MP on the brink of sexual diversions from the onerous task of governing the nation. And Joe now has a pair of glasses!

HUMFREY MALINS MP

I still play rugby so I was delighted that the whole rugby club *en masse* agreed to come canvassing during the last General Election. After three hours exhausting work, we met at the Conservative HQ. I asked the results of the canvass. The spokesman told me they had found four front row forwards, two scrum halves and a fullback -- the rest of my constituents did not play. I often wonder what effect this canvass had on the Election result!

DAVID BLUNKETT (Leader, Sheffield City Council)

I first stood for office as an elected representative in 1970 for Sheffield City Council at the age of 22. Very green, over-enthusiastic and not a little bumptious, I set out on my canvassing round. I was lucky; this was a safe Labour seat in the area in which I then lived with my mum. On the whole people were helpful and sympathetic, but the housing estate was like a nightmare for a visually handicapped door knocker.

Imagine having a guide dog and trying to get her to understand why it was that you had to go to doors which you didn't go in, but knocked and then went away. Ruby, who was then my guide dog, was a pedigree golden labrador. She was full of bounce, extremely intelligent and when she wasn't self-willed, full of initiative.

Ruby soon got the idea – down one path, negotiate a few often ill-repaired steps, round to the front door (which often was at the side of the house) and stop at the bottom whilst I negotiated where the door-knocker was. (In those days there were few door bells in the area I represented!)

The problem was not that Ruby didn't find the doors, it was explaining to her when the canvassing stopped. It would always take a few tentative false starts to get the canvassing started. We would miss a door or two, or we would wander up and down the hedge with me telling her to 'find the gate'. Sometimes we would hit a patch of open ground or an extensive corner plot which could be very frustrating! Sometimes we would miss a gate because there were two pathways alongside each other. Eventually she would get the idea and away we would go.

However, try explaining to a guide dog when you have finished canvassing and you want to carry on straight. Once she had got the 'bit between her teeth' she often felt that canvassing should continue regardless of my wishes. 'Straight up' I would instruct – which in English means forward straight along the pavement – no such luck, Ruby had decided that if canvassing it was, then canvassing it would be. We would end up in a ten minute battle between her going down pathways and me going straight on the pavement!

I always had a sneaking suspicion that she was politically keener than I was!

CROSSBENCHER (*Sunday Express*)

In the 1983 General Election, when Labour's publicity staff were looking around London for prominent poster sites, the head-quarters of the Post Office Engineering Union seemed an ideal spot.

It overlooked Hanger Lane on the busy A40 route into London. Hundreds of thousands of vehicles passed by every day. It could not be better placed.

Fired with enthusiasm, Labour art director Jack Stoddart set off for the POEU building with a van-load of equipment.

He spent endless hours inside, aligning a huge and imaginative display of posters along the interior of the windows which over-looked the busy thoroughfare. And at the end of his endeavours stepped outside to check the quality of his work.

Alas, alas. The glass of the POEU building is of a very special sort. You can see out. But no matter how hard you look, you can't see in.

RICHARD PAGE MP

The following was told to me about a candidate at a General Election standing for a Midlands seat. This candidate, a worthy but unexciting speaker, addressed the local residents' association. At the conclusion, he was escorted to the door by the chairman and on the way, they both clearly heard an old boy say: 'Boring, very boring.'

The chairman, trying to make amends, and all of a fluster, said to the speaker: 'Don't worry about old Smithers . . . he's going ga-ga – he just goes round repeating what everyone else is saying.'

ANONYMOUS MP

ITN sent a reporter, Geoffrey Archer, to do a street walkabout with each candidate. Just before Archer's arrival, my agent placed thirty known Conservatives at ten yard intervals down the High Street. With Archer and cameras I was taken down the street greeting these alleged strangers. Each met me with enthusiasm, applauded my campaign and said the Conservatives were doing brilliantly there. ITN were amazed and that night, Archer exclaimed on *News At Ten*: 'And there could yet be a surprise in this Labour stronghold.'

NICK COMFORT (*Daily Telegraph* Press Gallery)

A left-wing newspaper seller of my acquaintance found he could clear twenty copies by standing outside a tube station shouting: 'All the winners. All the winners. Marx, Lenin, Engles, Trotsky.'

He would then make a hasty getaway before the commuters realized they hadn't been sold copies of the racing final.

GEOFF ROBERTSON (BBC World Services)

I like the story about the Brecon and Radnor by-election. It comes from the *Wall Street Journal* and the last paragraph ended like this: 'As the day comes to an end, the hacks assembled at the Wellington Hotel wondering where the BBC's Vincent Hanna, the world's leading specialist in the coverage of by-elections, was. He and his crew, it turns out, have been chasing sheep across a meadow just outside the town. 'Vincent,' says a colleague, 'wants to line the sheep up for an interview.' Well, why not?

SIR JOHN JUNOR (Editor, *Sunday Express*)

I'm reminded of the canvassing story involving Sir Anthony Meyer who was accosted by a local resident. 'I'm 87,' said the man. Sir Anthony was about to tell his constituent that he didn't look a day over 75 when the man added: 'Yes and the chap in number 86 is going to vote for you, too.'

Half a second faster on his reply and the Meyer majority could well have been cut by one.

JOHN EVANS MP

I had shown a party of about thirty junior school children, from my St Helens constituency, round the House of Commons and then asked them into a committee room and given them a short lecture on the procedures of Parliament before inviting them to ask questions.

Quite a number did so, until finally, amid the sea of upturned little faces, a tough-looking 10-year-old asked me: 'Did you used to have a proper job before you came here?'

Sir Robin Day could scarcely have timed it to do more damage.

DENNIS SKINNER MP (Lab)

When campaigning during the South Wales Brecon and Radnor by-election last year, I bustled about a housing estate and was spotted by two men operating an ice cream van. The burly pair approached me, shook me warmly by the hand and offered me a swirling vanilla creation. 'It's on us,' they told me.

'Thanks a lot lads,' said I, not keen on payola, 'but I insist on paying.' But they wouldn't accept any money and off they trundled in their vehicle with a cheery wave. As the van turned the corner, it tinkled out not the normal nursery jingle but the unmistakable refrain of 'The Red Flag'.

The thought crossed my mind that perhaps the vendors were a couple of striking miners who'd moved from coal to cornets. They were.

MICK LUCKHURST (candidate's aide)

The keen young Liberal was persuasive on my doorstep and I invited him in to talk about the Liberal Party's policies. Two hours and several cups of tea later, there was a dramatic thrashing at my door knocker. An irate Liberal agent stood there. 'You clot,' he told his colleague, who had ventured out, hearing the commotion. 'He's chairman of the local Labour Party.'

JOHN WHITFIELD MP

When I first decided to stand for Parliament, I thought that the best place from which to start was in the constituency in which I lived. The fact that Hemsworth had one of the biggest Labour majorities anywhere in the UK did not deter me.

Immediately following my adoption meeting, at which I had made a suitably stirring speech, I organized a group of my still enthusiastic supporters to begin the campaign that very evening. Where better to start than the heart of my socialist constituency, which was the local dog track at Kinsley, where I knew a race meeting was being held that very night. With a group of six colleagues, each sporting a new royal blue rosette, I descended on the track. We paid the usual protection fee to the local mafia (small boys) who manned the car park and warned us that if we did not entrust our vehicles to their care they would undoubtedly come to some harm. We bought our tickets, went in and immediately began to canvass the punters.

The expression on the faces of the local miners, whose evening diversions were being disturbed by a swarm of Tory canvassers, had to be seen to be believed. Their jaws literally dropped wide open. They had never before seen a Tory candidate at their local greyhound stadium. Eventually one of the shocked punters pulled himself together and took me on one side to give me some advice. As Yorkshiremen tend to do, he came straight to the point. 'Now lad,' he told me 'You have got as much f...ing chance of getting voted in here as I have of nobbling the Pope's dog biscuits.'

I considered this assessment of my political prospects very carefully and came to the conclusion that from such a low point they could only move in an upwards direction.

RICHARD BALFE MEP (Lab)

In 1973 I stood for the GLC and was assisted by a gentleman who worked as a financier in the City of London. Apart from his pinstripes and bowler, which were like a red rag to a bull in a Labour district, he had also been to Eton and served in the Queen's Guards. His method of canvassing was to knock on the door and ask in a very 'plummy' voice, 'I wonder whether you would be good enough to tell me whether you will be supporting the candidate standing in my interest.' If they said 'yes', he marked them down as against and if they said 'piss off' he marked them down as a Labour voter. He always maintained that this method gave a far more accurate picture of how people would vote than the usual protestations and as it transpired he was right.

DERRICK MOLOCK (County Councillor)

Whilst 'knocking-up' in the closing minutes one polling day some years ago in municipal elections in Ramsgate, I called at a house where, according to the local Labour committee room records, all had voted except one.

When the door opened I was told that the voter in question, a young married lady, was about to have a bath and indeed I heard the sounds of water gurgling bath-wards upstairs.

Desperately I pleaded that it looked as if we had a chance in this previously held Tory seat provided we polled every available Labour vote and after a few minutes vocal exchange up and down stairs, a slightly reluctant young lady clad in bra, panties and dressing gown, plus bedroom slippers, descended and was bundled, albeit a little unceremoniously, into a waiting car.

The time was now 8.55pm and we reached the polling station

just as the doors were closing and squeezed her in with inches and just seconds to spare.

The result in that particular ward, finally announced after several recounts: a Labour gain from Conservative; majority, one vote!

GORDON WILSON MP (SNP)

During the February 1974 Election when I won the seat from Labour, an incident occurred which caused a flutter of alarm in our Campaign HQ.

A canvass in a particular housing scheme had shown a lot of support for the Scottish Nationalist Party: in the windows of all the houses along one major bus route, our posters bristled defiantly. One day, however, we looked along the serried ranks – and nearly every poster had been taken down. Fearing a strong Labour Party fightback a team of experienced canvassers was immediately dispatched to the area.

It turned out that Labour hadn't been at our posters at all. It was a team of window cleaners.

CROSSBENCHER (*Sunday Express*)

In the '83 election David Steel, the Liberal leader, found his entourage increased by two Special Branch 'shadows' as protection against a possible terrorist attack.

The two policemen posed an accommodation crisis for British Rail when Mr Steel caught an Edinburgh to London sleeper. The train was chock-full, with not a corner available for the two unexpected travellers.

A resourceful guard solved the problem by turfing two other passengers off the train to make room for Mr Steel's protectors.

An action which provoked consternation in the Steel party, until their anxieties were laid to rest.

The two unlucky passengers were only American tourists. Without a vote between them.

MATTHEW PARRIS MP (Cons)

When canvassing with a rather unethical colleague for a local government election, we were confronted by a gentleman who said he had heard that the Labour Party might introduce euthanasia for pensioners above a certain age, if they got back to power. I was about to reassure him that this was unthinkable, when my colleague intervened, 'I must be honest with you, sir. It is not in their manifesto at borough council level: but it is just the kind of thing they would do!'

I use this story when tutoring young Conservative canvassers as an example of an approach which I think goes beyond the bounds of what it is reasonable to do in the interests of the Party!

WILLIAM F. NEWTON DUNN MEP

I fought my first parliamentary election as a Conservative candidate in South Wales during the 1974 miners strike. I had a new chairman at the start of the campaign. But my canny agent, who had fought the seat himself, believed the chairman was only doing the job in order to obtain the then-usual MBE. The agent decided to make the chairman earn his medal – and sent him out with me to canvass in the mining villages.

The chairman assured me he knew what he was doing – and I naturally followed his lead. After knocking on a few doors, we felt that our reception had been surprisingly friendly: the only repeatedly negative comment was that I did not look like my photograph in the election address.

Despite our jokes about never looking like one's passport photograph, one Welsh lady insisted – and fetched the election address.

There could be no doubt about it: the photo was not mine. We were canvassing in the neighbouring constituency. Welsh communities are very close. I lost the election and so did my neighbour.

JOHN CARTWRIGHT MP

When I had a complaint from a newly built council estate that the authorities were refusing to remove a dead horse from the rear of their homes, within hours I managed, through some personal contacts, to get the corpse decently removed. I thought no more about it. But a year later, during the General Election campaign, I was all the rage and found that the tenants greeted me, not as SDP founder or Labour defector. I was simply 'the man who shifted the dead horse'. Which only goes to prove that it does sometimes pay to flog a dead horse.

HELEN WILLIAMS (activist)

Canvasser to voter: 'Would you like to meet your candidate?'
    'No, thank you.'
    'I knew you would . . . come with me.'

MICHAEL BLOND

A parliamentary candidate was desperate to get some television coverage and approached all the TV stations telling them he was available any time of the day or night to talk about absolutely anything. Eventually, he received a letter from a TV company asking if he could appear on a particular programme and if a fee of £50 was acceptable. He wrote back by return: 'I accept and my cheque for £50 is enclosed.'

'My next guest . . . an MP I managed to lure here tonight . . .'

JOHN WARDEN (Political Editor, *Daily Express*)

A delicate young woman candidate on her first campaign ran into an abusive and hostile elector who let forth an earful, climaxing with the epithet '******* Tory'.

Not being much used to that sort of thing, the young lady rather lost her composure. Still shaken, she moved to the next house and was horrified to hear herself say, 'I am your ****** Tory candidate.'

ROBERT TYRRELL (activist)

Canvasser (on council house doorstep): 'Good evening. I'm canvassing on behalf of the local Liberal candidate, and I wonder if you could give me some indication of whether you might be supporting him in the forthcoming election.'

Woman: 'No, no – we all vote Labour in this house.'

Canvasser: 'Fine, thank you for your help. Goodbye.'

Woman: 'But I hope your man gets in.'

This tale always seemed to me to epitomise the British voter, attitudes to the Liberal Party and the surrealism of politics in general.

PETER McCAIG

It was with some apprehension that I accepted nomination as a political candidate in the recent County Council elections.

It was one thing to overcome the hurdle of the initial selection meeting. Here one at least faced a panel of people with common political sympathies. Canvassing – the now essential 'knocking on doors' (particularly since the virtual demise of the public meeting in local elections) – was quite another matter.

Perhaps my first surprise was to find the quite considerable number of doors which had neither knockers nor bells – and some without letterboxes. (Whatever does the postman do in such circumstances?) I certainly would never have believed the variety of electric bell sounds, from the conventional ting-a-ling to quite exotic harmonies, some of them lasting up to a minute or so. It was surprising also to note the number of houses (much more so in the case of shops) which had no number or other means of postal identification on them, although every now and then the householder displayed some ingenuity, such as the LVI on the house between numbers 54 and 58. That probably foxed the postman all right.

I sometimes found quite risky the simple operation of pushing the candidate's leaflet through the letterbox amid sounds of murderous growling and snarling – and just escaping with five unscathed fingers. I also found out that a number of letterboxes had razor sharp edges – and were often spring-loaded. I took with me a supply of elastoplast after my first accident.

Of course it's the people that provide the unforgettable experiences. The generally nice but somewhat non-committed men and women of Britain who accept your approach in a pleasant enough manner, the more explicit of whom either shake your hand or would like to shake your neck. I experienced very little verbal abuse although some made it quite clear that no politicians of any sort would get their vote.

One or two inevitable surprises. The opening of a number of front doors to reveal ladies in various stages of undress (I wasn't quite sure whether I had interrupted anything special), the young husband and wife in the hallway both bottle feeding their (presumably) twin infants and the Mr MacLeod (the Scots clan of which McCaig is a subordinate part) who turned out to be black!

Only a pedometer could confirm the mileage involved in the walking up and down of individual pathways (not risking the loss of potential votes by crossing trim lawns) and the upstairs/downstairs ordeal of so many stairs in those apparently interminable blocks of flats. But I walked a marathon during those three weeks of canvassing and have the blisters to prove it.

When I said 'yes' to that invitation to contest the County Council seat I didn't realize what an eye-opener it would be. I wasn't the successful candidate but I found it all part of life's rich pattern.

MICHAEL MEACHER MP

The most succinct letter I have ever received followed a press release I gave concerning the effects of Mrs Thatcher's government cuts since 1979. I stated that Mrs T's message to the poor, if it were frankly stated, could only be 'drop dead'.

The letter I received said simply: 'Dear Michael, Drop dead.'

ALASDAIR HUTTON MEP

One thing a candidate dreads during a hard campaign is being kept up late by an enthusiastic host. But having an invisible host who makes no demands at all can be equally disconcerting.

Arriving late one night at the country house of a benevolent supporter, my agent and I found the front door open, the lights on, a tray of refreshments in the hall with an invitation to help ourselves – but no people. After a long pause while we wondered what to do, we climbed the stairs and found two rooms with bedlights and electric blankets on.

In the morning there was still no sign of a soul, only a note asking us to sign the Visitors' Book before we went.

It was like Close Encounters – of the invisible kind.

15
The Good Old Days

BARONESS BIRK JP

Many years ago when I was canvassing in Portsmouth West and was a young and beautiful red-headed candidate, I was electioneering one day and stopped by a huge dustcart with two hefty young men standing on top. One jumped down and said, 'Is it true that candidates kiss babies?' 'Oh yes,' I said beaming, whereupon the other young man jumped down and the first one said, 'Well, will you kiss my baby brother then?' Which I did.

At a meeting one evening I was taking questions after I had spoken, and one of the audience asked me something to which I replied, 'I'm very sorry, I don't know the answer.' He applauded and said 'wonderful'. I thought perhaps he was being sarcastic, but afterwards he came up to me and said that that was the first time he had ever heard a candidate honest enough to admit to not knowing all the answers. 'I salute you for that,' he said. 'Although I am a Liberal I will vote for you.'

NEIL KINNOCK MP

Labour standard bearers in rural Tory redoubts have seen the wrong end of shotguns and been chased by dogs. Conversely, in a South Wales mining seat half a century ago, an amazed Conservative candidate was chaired from a tumultuous meeting by cheering miners. Delighted by the reception, he called to one of those carrying him that he was grateful, but that he'd like to return to his car. 'Car be damned,' said the miners, 'we're taking you to the river.'

There were gentler welcomes. My mother – a tungsten-coated

socialist – used to make a practice of using a Tory car to take her to the polling booth, kindly inviting the driver in for a cup of tea and keeping him talking for anything up to an hour on the tactical grounds that 'while he's taking my tea, he's not taking anyone else's votes.'

ROY HATTERSLEY MP

After he had retired from active politics, the phlegmatic ex-Prime Minister Clement Atlee was once canvassed by some keen Labour supporters. They spent some minutes telling him the advantages of voting for their candidate. Clement looked, listened, then puffed on his pipe before he told them: 'Already a member.' And shut the door.

VIC TURTON (former Lord Mayor of Birmingham and Labour County Councillor)

After the war, when houses were scarcer than fresh meat, a woman came to my advice bureau every Friday for eighteen months pleading to be rehoused. She wept; she stormed. Her plight was extremely touching and I made up my mind to help her. Finally, through a great deal of effort and by being repaid for every favour I'd ever done, I managed to get this lady what she so desperately wanted – a new home. At the next election, I knocked on her door to ask – just out of politeness really – whether she'd be voting for me. 'Not bloody likely,' she replied, 'You kept me waiting a whole 18 months for a house.'

BRYAN GOULD MP

I like the election story involving Lady Astor, the first woman to be elected to Parliament. While out canvassing in the less salubrious districts of Devonport, she was accompanied by a high-ranking naval officer for protection. Knocking at one of the doors in such an area, Lady Astor was confronted by a little girl. 'Is your mother at home?' enquired Lady Astor. To which the child replied: 'No she isn't. But she told me that if a lady and a sailor arrived, I was to show them the front room and say it'll be one and sixpence, please.'

CHARLES JAMES (activist)

My favourite election character was a fanatical Socialist in Chester whose name was Harry. He'd been on the General Strike Committee in Salford in 1926 and as a member of Manchester City Council, had appalled fellow members by shouting out, upon the formal report to the Council of the death of a Tory Alderman: 'Another Labour gain!' He was involved in the 1919 Election when the Conservative slogan was that they would 'squeeze the Kaiser till the pips squeaked'. He argued that they wouldn't because the Kaiser was too closely related to the Royal Family. The police had to rescue him from being thrown into the canal.

Once he persuaded a friend who owned an ice cream van to fix the chimes so it played 'Vote for a Rent Rise, Vote Conservative'!

But the best story about him refers to his time as a trade union official. He sent his number three into a factory to negotiate union recognition but the management refused to see him. The number two was then sent in and the same thing happened. So Harry took both these men into the factory and saw the manager. Two hours later he came out and said: 'We're recognized, lads, but by God he's stubborn. I had to hit him.'

SIR ROBIN DAY

In the 1964 General Election, the BBC invited viewers to send in questions for the three party leaders to answer. This was for the programme *Election Forum*. My exchange with the-then leader of the Conservative Party went as follows:

RD: Sir Alec Douglas-Home, our first question comes from a lady in Curzon Street who wants you to know that if you lose the Election, it won't be because of your smile, which she finds much more warm and attractive than Mr Wilson's. What have you got to say about that?'

SIR ALEC: 'I think she must be the only lady in Curzon Street whom I do not know.'

Mean Streets

(Punch, 8 June 1983)

JONATHAN SALE under canvass

Sir Robin Day was not there to report the event, the *Daily Express* was not there to misreport it and Stock Exchange figures did not tremble as a result of what took place. But to the small group in the meeting, or rather, hanging about outside on the pavement on the off-chance that someone would turn up with the key to the room, it was a sign that the Election campaign was hotting up in a big way.

'Good God,' the cry went up from the wind-swept band, 'Jonathan's coming to a Labour Party ward meeting!'

Election Fever Sweeps South London – Latest. It was at the time when Mrs Thatcher was dithering towards her decision to go to the country that it dawned on me that the inmates currently running the asylum might possibly be asked to carry on dispensing the rubber waistcoats and plugging in the cranial cattle-prods.

There was nothing for it. I blew the dust off my Labour Party membership card and reported for duty. By waiting on the street corner, and indeed going in when the key duly arrived, I made what could be called, if I knew what the words meant, a quantum leap. I leapt with one bound from 92% of the population to an elite 8%, from an ordinary suburban householder to an opinion-former before whom multinationals mind their manners. MORI says so.

Polling organisations are like Father Christmas; they swing into the public's consciousness for a brief period and sink from view for lengthy intervals. But just as Santa Claus is hard at it making toys for his next delivery date, so market research companies pay the rent by conducting in-depth research on what sort of toothpaste middle-class housewives in Midlothian prefer to eradicate Mars Bar leftovers from their children's molars.

In the case of Market Opinion Research International, '95% of our research is attitudinal rather than behavioural.' A random sample of one *Punch* journalist failed to follow that, so the MORI spokesman kindly translated it as 'We are concerned with what people think rather than what they do. We examine what people think of a company's image rather than its product.'

To enable a company to address itself to the people who affect other people's views, MORI *could* prepare a neatly typed statement bound in red, nearly-leather folder and tied with a pink ribbon to the effect that: 'We happen to know a loud-mouth in the saloon bar of the Mucky Duck who will prove that black is white in the time it takes to catch the barman's eye for a double-whisky and whatever-you're-having. Get him on your side and the world's your oyster.' I could name a market research organisation which would do little more than that, and charge a prince's ransom for it.

What MORI has done is to pin-point 'the political/social leaders in our community' according to the 'activist scale developed at the Opinion Research Corporation in Princeton, New Jersey'. To become an activist it is necessary to be able to score five out of the following ten:

'Made a speech before an organised group.' 14% of the sample had got on their hind legs in this context, as opposed to 71% of activists. (0% of me has achieved that.)

'Stood for public office.' 1% of the population does that but 8% of activists put their names forward to an electorate of one sort or another. (And I sit that one out.)

'Been elected an officer of an organisation or club.' 14% of the population managed that, 65% of activists. (To paraphrase the political thoughts of Marx – Groucho – I wouldn't join a club shaky enough to have me as its treasurer.)

'Written a letter to an editor.' 6% managed that, but if you stopped a hundred activists in the street, you would find thirty-five of them had recently put pen to paper. (Not me though, unless you count missives to the editor of this publication, to the effect that Dear Sir, I have gone out for the afternoon and my article is in the oven.)

But to 'Presented my views to a local councillor or MP' (13% of total, 65% of activists); 'Urged someone outside my family to vote' (17% and 68%); 'Urged someone to get in touch with a local councillor or MP' (17% and 78%); 'Taken an active part in a political campaign' (3% and 28%); and 'Helped on fund raising drives' (31% and 85%), to all those, I can qualify by answering as I would have replied if stopped by MORI pollsters gathering information at the end of last year, with a more or less enthusiastic Yes. As I would have done to the question that elicited the highest percentage from both total (69%) and activist (95%) sectors: 'Voted in the last election'. Mind you, I don't know what kind of activists they can call themselves in the missing five per cent, if they are too inactive to put their cross in the electoral ballot.

You don't have to be sitting next to me at a Labour Party meeting to count as an activist. Far from it, I am sorry to say. Scratch a hundred activists (gently, or they will write to the papers about it) and 25% of them will be Labour, 41% Conservative and 20% Alliance (or Don't Knows, as we say in the trade).

When not writing to the papers, we read them, at least 81% of us do, 31% of us read the 'quality press', as opposed to 11% of 'non-activists', which raises our general tone. It is lowered again by the astonishing 13% of us who read *The Sun* (not broken down into those who do and don't move their lips the while); the consolation is that twice as many non-activists take it, which could explain their lack of activity.

There is more to us than our score on the activity scale. There is also the question of where we rate in terms of ACORN. This is nothing to do with living in the middle of a wood (although 'villages with non-farm employment' come into the equation). If you give, as I did, your postcode to C.A.C.I. Market Analysis Division, you can discover where you stand, and indeed live, in terms of 'A Classification Of Residential Neighbourhoods'.

'You,' the ACORN lady told me as she tapped out London SE23 3RA on her computer, 'are what we call "Type F20". Previously you were "I32", before being reclassified.'

The first turns out to stand for 'Inter-war council estates, older people' and the second 'Furnished flats, mostly single people'. Neither of those labels applies to property on the street where live, but both cover the nearby roads up which I plod and on the front doors of which I knock politely to make sure no one is going to be loopy enough to put votes Mrs Thatcher's way.

C.A.C.I. Market Analysis Division do not produce these letters and numerals for fun. ACORN is 'a marketing segmentation system which enables consumers to be classified according to the type of residential area in which they live'. There is no point, for example, in having people push leaflets about double-glazing through the letter-boxes of anywhere with a postcode that registers as G18. This signifies 'Small council estates, often Scottish', which means that the local authority would make the necessary decision, that is, no; it does not mean that sometimes the estate moves into Scotland and sometimes it stays where it is, but that a high proportion are situated North of the Border. I think. The man from MORI had spent some time explaining the simplest statistical point, before remarking consolingly that several of his clients had proved slower on the uptake than me God, help the poor fellow.

'Poor Asians, multi-occupied terraces' what market researchers find in H26 'These immigrants live together at very high occupancies. Overcrowding reaches levels experienced only in the very worst Clydeside overspill estates.' Fighting words, that could have come out of Marx-Karl – but have a less revolutionary message: Don't push leaflets through the communal letter-boxes advertising Porsches or schemes to finance private education Smarties, perhaps: 'The ratio of pre-school children to pensioners is five times the national average.'

A Lotus is parked outside the part of the ACORN guide for I30 – 'High-status non-family areas'. 45% of households run one car, Lotus or otherwise, 15% two. 15% walk to work, which may be of interest to shoe manufacturers, while 1½% do not run to a bath, despite their high status, and the same again have to go outside for the lavatory.

B7 sounds promising. 31% walk to work but 'Incomes and car ownership are above average. There is a fairly high expenditure on consumer goods and family leisure activities.' There are 1.6 rooms per person and a mere half of a per cent have no bath. It sounds a promising market.

But take care as you tramp around in the dusk pushing things under doors. B7 is the codeword for 'Military bases' and the authorities may be curious about your activity. Remember, too, that although 'target' is the expression for the consumers at whom products are aimed it may have a more literal meaning to men behind triggers in another power bloc.

LADY FALKENDER

When Labour was fighting the 1970 Election, I had trouble with television over Harold Wilson's speaking engagements in the south-west. I rang the BBC to ask how they were going to cover one of his speeches. The reply – in carefully chosen words I'm sure – was that at the time of speaking to me, they were in the process of erecting a scaffold for him outside the committee room windows.

Many electors knew how they felt. We lost that election.

DAVID HARRIS MP

At the end of a meal, the Earl of Longford and the-then Prime Minister Clement Attlee found they hadn't enough cash to pay for the lunch. Mr Attlee commented: 'I could pay by cheque – the trouble is, I'm not known here.'

SIR LARRY LAMB (former Editor, *Daily Express*)

This is the story of James Margach's debut in the Commons Press Gallery. In nearly fifty years at Westminster, Margach became the doyen of the Lobby journalists.

But he arrived as a novice in the Thirties when Ramsay MacDonald was Prime Minister. It was an astute move by his editor in Aberdeen because Margach had covered MacDonald's home town of Lossiemouth, and knew him well.

The young reporter took his seat in the Press Gallery, looking down on the Front Bench. The Prime Minister gave a nod of recognition. After question-time Margach was taken aside by a very superior Gallery man and given a short and disdainful lecture on the rules and etiquette of reporting Parliament.

'I wonder,' ventured the newcomer politely, 'could you kindly show me the way to the Prime Minister's room?'

'Oh, but you don't just walk in there, son.'

'Well, I've been invited for tea with the Prime Minister,' said Margach, waving a note he had been handed.

Nothing like it had been heard of before. An audience with the Prime Minister. The grandees of the Press Gallery, in their striped pants, went into a huddle to wonder about this phenomenon in the tweed jacket. They waited for young Margach to return.

'What did Mr MacDonald say?' they chorused.

'Oh, this and that,' replied Margach. 'Tell me, can I get a tram to Chequers?'

GEOFFREY GOODMAN (Mirror Newspapers)

My story concerns Harold Wilson in 1964. I had been with him throughout the election campaign and was on the train from Liverpool that memorable Friday morning when he was being called to the Palace. It was belatedly realized that to present himself to Her Majesty as Britain's potential Prime Minister, he would need morning clothes, suitable shirt and tie to match. Which he did not possess. So when we arrived at Euston he dispatched Alf Richman (*Daily Herald*) to a local gent's outfitters to buy him a few bits of clothing so that he could go to the Palace. (I think Alf paid for these out of his own pocket.)

When we got to Transport House, then the party headquarters, I was due to interview Wilson for the *Daily Herald*, which I did, in a first floor room while he was changing to go to the Palace! Indeed, it was the first interview with the new Prime Minister. I remember he kept looking at his watch because he was already late for the Queen. Suddenly he discovered he had no braces to go with his newly acquired morning clothes. The much put-upon Alf Richman was once again dispatched to a shop to buy the Prime Minister a pair of braces. Red, of course.

WINIFRED EWING MEP

In 1968 as the new MP for Hamilton, winning the seat at a much-publicised by-election, I was invited to be a guest at a Press Gallery luncheon, a much coveted type of invitation to MPs. I found myself the sole woman present. The occasion was to thank Emmanuel Shinwell for forty years in the House.

At the end of the lunch all present lined up to shake his hand. As the only woman there I felt I had to do something more significant to mark the occasion so I said, 'I think I will give you a kiss.' At this the 78-year-old peer brushed me aside refusing my gesture and this was for the moment rather humiliating as there was a considerable audience of all the Press. The late Lord Shinwell, as he later became, added: 'What use is one kiss to me? It's all or nothing.'

LORD CHAMPION

Lord Haldane had developed something of a pot which Churchill, then a rather brash young Cabinet colleague, poked with his finger and asked Haldane what he was going to call it. Haldane replied: 'If it's a boy, I shall name him George after the King. If it's a girl, after Her Majesty the Queen. But if it's only wind, I shall call it Winston.'

PETER PRESTON (Editor, *The Guardian*)

There's no substitute for meeting the people; but no substitute either for meeting the candidates. I spent a couple of years on the election circuit twenty or more years ago and the memories are gently ludicrous rather than funny ha-ha. The Liberal candidate in Derby who retired to his sofa each night to listen to the Archers 'so that I can go after the farming vote'; Mr Frank Cousins in Nuneaton gabbling bad-temperedly through the issued text of a speech so that he'd actually say what his campaign managers had said he'd say; the SNP candidate in Roxburgh who extolled the virtues of South African oranges; the Labour candidate in Dundee who wanted the town made a pedestrian precinct but then wandered into the most terrible maze when Mr A. J. Travers of the *Daily Telegraph* (print journalism's original Vincent Hanna) asked him how a doctor would get to a city centre heart attack.

But the oddest experience of the lot was the 1964 General Election. I was delegated to follow Jo Grimond, the Liberal Leader, every step of the way. Not many had that task; most swiftly vanished, including any permanent help for Jo from Liberal HQ. So, willy-nilly, because I was with him, I found myself carrying the bags and checking arrangements as he swept around one of the two Liberal heartlands of the time – the Highlands of Scotland. It was a fine, sunny morning in Dingwall, the throbbing heart of Ross and Cromarty. Our car – a little behind time – swept into the market place where Jo was scheduled to walk about and pump hands. A lot of farmers; a lot of sheep; not an identifiable Liberal in sight. I suggested that Jo go down to the local hotel and skulk quietly while I found what on earth was going on. Then I pottered round the square and found one ancient man in dirty trenchcoat with a battered pork pie hat.

'Can you tell me where the Liberals are?' Much Highland spluttering of a completely uncertain nature. 'Where's Mr Mackenzie, the Liberal candidate?' The old head nodded furiously: 'That's me, sonny. That's me.' Suddenly Orpington Man was a million miles away. He whistled, and people stopped talking and emerged from the cattle pens. I scuttled away to get Jo, writing off Ross and Cromarty as I went. A fortnight later, sitting back in London as the results came out, there he was. Mackenzie, A., duly declared elected. I'm not sure anyone at Westminster ever quite understood a word he said. But he'd a wonderful way with sheep.

BERNARD WEATHERILL MP (Mr Speaker)

At the time of the General Election in 1910, *The Sphere* had an article in which it was recommended that the electorate should look not only at the candidates' election addresses, but they should also note carefully the candidate's election dress! The article said:

'Georgiana, Duchess of Devonshire, kissed a drayman and got his vote. How she was attired when canvassing is not recorded – but she was probably wearing a large hat and expensive furs. Lady canvassers should wear things both passionate and dangerous. Depth and conviction lie in the brims of large hats. Lady canvassers should be attired so that they can be seen coming; they should invariably cause fluttered feelings or they are not doing their best. No election agent is a good one unless he chooses lady canvassers who know how to dress themselves . . .' It concluded:

CANVASSING

THE DEPUTATION

THE SUCCESSFUL
CANDIDATE

THE HUSTINGS

THE PUBLIC DINNER

It's all been said before
(Punch, 17 July 1841)

'Men in public life ought to give a lead. It is well known that a tidy-minded man dresses in a tidy way and that women are influenced greatly by the way a man dresses. They have an innate distrust of the man who slops about in non-pressed trousers and worn-out jackets. This is pure laziness, and women know it.

The implications are plain to see, dear reader: Beware the shabby candidates' shabby tricks. Beware that he with the turned coat be not a potential turn-coat. Beware that the fellow with the bad hat may well turn out to be one.'

16
Suffering Spouses and Children Plus Some Put-Upon PA's

DENIS THATCHER

I am afraid I cannot add to your collection for my sense of humour gets strained to breaking point during elections! Too many people know my 'classic'. Margaret holding a three-hour-old calf and my comment: 'Unless she's f--- careful we'll have a dead calf on our hands!'

GLENYS KINNOCK

In the 1964 election Neil and I were drenched by a bucket of window washing water thrown by a lady screaming her hatred of Jehovah's Witnesses. Both of us couldn't help being amused by this. When I laughingly explained that we weren't from the *Watchtower* but from the Labour Party I was set upon by the outraged lady with a wet chamois leather.

POLLY CORBETT (aged 11)

While out canvassing in Erdington, Birmingham for my Dad when I was 9, I approached a middle-aged woman looking at a piece of paper. Putting on my sweetest smile and opening my eyes very wide, I asked: 'Will you be voting Labour?'
'No,' she snapped, 'I'm voting for the Tories.'
As she walked away I crept up behind her and stuck twenty 'Vote for Corbett' stickers all down the back of her coat. Maybe it convinced her because we won that election!

JOHN HANNAM MP (Cons)

In 1974 my young daughter aged 13 desperately wanted to help her daddy in his election campaign, so off she set on the trail with the candidate's personal 'knocking-up' party. After behaving impeccably for an hour following quietly behind the helpers, Amanda asked if she could go solo and ventured alone up the pathways. Permission was given and in the next street off she went. Suddenly a look of horror froze Dad's face as he espied his young daughter knocking earnestly on the front door of a house which at first-floor level was festooned with 'Labour Committee Room' signs. A lady appeared at the door and engaged my child in deep conversation. Everyone waited for a tearful, fleeing return but back she came, smiling broadly, having been deep into enemy territory and sprayed the opposition with various Tory leaflets.

Either the Labour lady had very graciously kept mum, or my daughter should run for Prime Minister.

MAUREEN FITZ-HENRY (PA to Robin Corbett MP)

It was such a safe Labour constituency that the local Party had not done any canvassing for many years, on the grounds that the residents didn't like people knocking on their doors! So when they had a new enthusiastic Labour candidate, canvassing the area was new both for him and his party workers. Although he was liked very much no-one knew a great deal about him personally, and we were all interested to see how he went about winning votes.

The candidate knocked on the first door to be greeted by a lady and a boxer dog. He immediately bent down, stroked the dog, and told its owner 'What a lovely dog, I've one just like it at home.' A few doors down the road, a man came to the door with a Yorkshire terrier.

'What a lovely dog, I've one just like it at home.' During the course of the day the canvassing team found he also had an alsatian, a poodle, a pekinese and a collection of mongrels. Some thought he was an amazing dog-lover, but most were convinced he lived in Battersea Dogs Home.

L. ROBINSON (secretary to Greg Knight MP)

Derby North MP Greg Knight was canvassing for the Conservative candidate in one of the Leicester seats in the 1970 election. He was in the loudspeaker car which was approaching the-then stadium used for greyhound racing when a pedestrian suddenly ran out into the path. Through the loudspeaker, Mr Knight asked: 'Have you been to vote, sir?' To which the startled pedestrian shouted back: 'I can't be bothered, I'm going to the dogs.'

Without hesitation, Mr Knight reposted: 'The whole country's going to the dogs, so vote Conservative!' – which was greeted by a round of applause from a queue waiting at the bus stop.

EILEEN WRIGHT (PA to Matthew Parris MP)

In my nearly forty years here I have seen several elections come and go. I only went electioneering once, though, the rest of the time I have made sure I am in the office!

My first – and last – tramping of doorsteps was in 1959. I was 'helping' a candidate near a provincial airport. I did not want to go with him at all, but I was made to carry his literature so that he could pump hands. He would bound up to the door, knock firmly and wait. As soon as the occupant came to the door a large jet would roar overhead and the two would be left standing there gazing at one another and unable to say anything for the engine noise. It happened every time. Meanwhile, I was busy holding my sides with laughter and trying to hide round evergreen hedges as this pantomime was performed at every home. I was never asked again!

VAL HUDSON (Mrs Robin Corbett MP)

Just to prove that politicians live in another world . . . a week ago, on a rare Saturday off duty, my MP husband actually accompanied me to the supermarket. Because the checkouts were quite busy, I decided to use those at the back of the store, near the car park exit. Robin looked around wildly, after we'd paid: 'Where's the exit?' he asked. 'How do we get out?' I saw the supermarket cashier look at him oddly and I put on a concerned expression. 'Don't worry about him,' I said. 'He's just out of prison and finds it hard to accustom to life outside.' She looked at him with pity but with no hint of surprise: 'That explains it, then,' she said and went back to her till.

TIM BRINTON MP (Cons)

Question: 'Mrs Brinton, have you any special hints for election-eering wives?'
Answer: 'Yes, they should all carry a candidate's survival kit'.
Question: 'And what would that be?'
Mrs Brinton rummages in her handbag with gestures not dissimilar to the Prime Minister at the despatch box and extracts a sponge bag.
Answer: 'This is it. In here I keep a town map of Gravesend; some deodorant; smelling salts, and a corkscrew.' These would be invaluable if you were lost, hot, unconscious, four sheets to the wind or four square to the Labour Party HQ.

MARY CORMACK (Mrs Patrick Cormack MP)

Very little is sacred in a Member's life but as far as we are concerned Sundays are. It is not that we are an excessively pious family but we do like to be together on that day and from the moment my husband entered the House he steadfastly refused to undertake any Sunday engagements other than the annual civic service and the Remembrance Day parade.

Callers are definitely discouraged. If they come, then the white protective lie is used unless there really is an emergency. The visit one Sunday in May some four years ago did not fall into this category. Mr 'Furious South Staffordshire' was aggrieved that the local council had turned down a planning application and was determined to see the Member. He called just as we sat down to Sunday lunch and so I was not in the best of humours when I went to the door. Nevertheless he was neither easily fobbed off nor offensive and as the silent family realized that I was having a fairly long altercation Patrick decided he had better attend to the vegetables. His problem was that if he emerged from the dining room it would be quite obvious that he was not out of the country and so he decided to negotiate the serving hatch. As he emerged into the kitchen he looked out of the window and there, sitting in a very large motorcar and looking straight in, were the complainant's wife and mother-in-law.

Patrick's secretary received a charming and reassuring telephone call from the wife the next morning to say that she would not tell, and indeed she said she had informed her husband that he was driving her mad with his persistence and if he did not drop the wretched application she would drop him!

MAUREEN FITZ-HENRY (PA to Robin Corbett MP)

We were bravely campaigning for Labour in a traditional Tory neighbourhood, but without much success, until at last one man was actually prepared to listen and we went into our spiel.

At the end of it, we waited, hearts in our mouths. 'Yes, very interesting, but it doesn't affect me because I have my own business,' he said. This gave us a life line. How many small businesses, we asked, were going downhill since the Tories came into power? How many were going into *bankruptcy* each year? This must win him over, we thought. But no. He sympathized with businesses that were finding it tough, but had to tell us that his own business was doing very well. And what business was that, we asked cynically.

'I'm a liquidator.'

I knocked on one house of a family of seven voters, all of whom regularly voted Labour. The door opened. No carpets on the floor and packing cases everywhere. The father was very sorry that he could not vote for Jo Richardson this last time but he was moving out the next day. 'If they were moving somewhere in the district, would the family come back to vote on Election Day?' 'Very sorry but it just wasn't possible'. I wasn't going to lose seven Labour votes without a struggle, so I told him if he'd let me have their new address I'd arrange for postal votes to be sent to them. For a supporter he seemed very doubtful if this was possible, but I finally convinced him and he gave me his new address – Jamaica, West Indies.

JUNE SHARMAN (Constituency PA to Patrick Cormack MP)

One of my duties during the last General Election was to ensure that the candidate visited all the committee rooms at least once on election day.

I telephoned one branch to say that the candidate would visit them at 6.30 the next day (which seemed to me a good time to catch the evening rush). When I got to the office the following morning a very irate lady telephoned to ask where was the candidate? She and her other friends had risen at 5.00am in order to pretty themselves up and open the committee room to show how bright-eyed and bushy-tailed they were and they were still waiting – bleary-eyed and bushwacked. I'm afraid they still haven't forgiven me to this day.

MRS NICHOLAS EDWARDS

Our first election in Pembrokeshire was in June 1970. The temperature was 80 degrees and I was six-and-a-half months pregnant. Our first meeting of the evening was in the City Hall, St Davids (a modest village hall not to be confused with the fine concert hall in Cardiff). The local chairman had recently had a heart attack, but pills in hand, he started to preside. During his opening remarks, a noisy group of enthusiastic Welsh Nationalists trouped in and sat in the front row. They heckled my husband throughout his speech, but hadn't reckoned on his very loud Albert Hall voice. He didn't give way for an instant. The Chairman's face grew redder and redder and I was terrified he would have another heart attack before our very eyes.

As I was sitting immediately behind the hecklers, I grabbed my neighbour's walking stick and started banging them all on the head, whispering 'quiet, quiet!' My husband looked aghast; the agent thunderstruck – what would be the headlines in the local papers? 'Candidate's wife assaults hecklers!'

For the remainder of the campaign, two strong men sat on either side of me at every meeting – their arms tightly linked in mine.

VAL HUDSON (Mrs Robin Corbett MP)

Canvassing with my husband in Hertfordshire one sunny Sunday morning, we came across a most beautiful manor house with a winding, wooded driveway. 'Let's skip this one,' I suggested, with my mind on other things, like lunch. But my husband, in the vanguard of Socialism, was not that easily dissuaded.

As we approached the house, I took care to place myself behind him so he would take the full brunt of whatever was about to fall about our ears. In the event, the sound of clicking high heels prefaced an elegantly dressed woman with a sherry glass who, on hearing who we were, said: 'But how too, too terribly nice of you to take the trouble of calling on us . . . do come in and have a sherry.' Then she called to her husband: 'Darling, come down, you'll never guess in a fit who's here.'

Leading us into the drawing room, she said: 'Of course, we're not of your political persuasion . . .' Robin murmured: 'Where there's life, there's hope.' Pouring the sherry, she continued: 'You see, I am a member of the Workers' Revolutionary Party, my husband is a Communist but my son is *flirting* with the Labour Party, so you may be lucky there.'

AN MP'S SECRETARY

His was a marginal constituency and a TV crew came up to accompany him on his canvassing rounds. Knocking on several doors, all seemed to go well. Then he came to an elderly lady who chatted to him for several minutes about her support for him. 'Well,' he said, 'is there anything particular troubling you at present?' She thought for a moment while the cameras whirred. 'Ee, laddie,' she said, 'It's me back.'

The candidate, returned again as the MP, wouldn't allow the TV people to use that interchange, despite it being the high point of his campaign.

AN MP'S SECRETARY

We were getting pretty punch-drunk towards the end of the campaign. It was the day before polling when the candidate was walking down the main shopping precinct, stopping every now and then to talk to people. Suddenly, he turned and waved merrily at what I thought was a shop window. We went a few paces on and I asked who he'd waved to. 'The fellow in there,' he replied.

When we looked, the 'fellow' turned out to be a cardboard cutout of comedian Harry Worth raising his hat and inviting customers into the shop.

TIM RENTON MP

My wife and I were canvassing together. She rang the doorbell. The door was opened by a young wife who, after hearing who my wife was, pointed to the small twins playing around her feet and said, 'I am so pleased to meet you. I would never have had these without your husband's help.'

TIM BRINTON MP

In 1979, faced for the umpteenth time with a constituent who stopped my wife in the street to ask for my views on abortion, the death penalty and pornography (Catholic priests had instructed their flock from the pulpit to question all candidates on these matters), Jeanne replied: 'Tim would like to ease the abortion laws; he'd like to reintroduce the death penalty and pornography? Oh yes, Tim's all in favour of that.'

And I still got re-elected!

NICHOLAS BAKER MP

My wife Carol was asked to go and call on a lady who had a particularly confidential matter she wished to discuss. Carol duly called on the lady who took the greatest care to see that no-one in the street was within earshot before she put her question.

'Is it true,' she asked Carol, 'that the Queen has changed her account from Harrods to Peter Jones?'

17
Let's Hear it for the Old Biddies

CHARLES JAMES (activist)

One of my favourite canvassing stories concerns an old lady in the early seventies who was asked why she voted Labour.

'What, dear?' said the old lady, her head vibrating gently from side to side.

'We wondered why *Labour* had always *got your vote*,' said the canvasser, enunciating clearly.

'Got my goat?'

'Your *vote*. Why have you always been a Labour supporter?' mouthed the canvasser.

'Oh vote!' she sucked her gums ruminatively. 'Well, it was Labour that brought in the free hearing aids, you see. Before that, we had ear trumpets.'

ROBERT RHODES-JAMES MP

This is supposed to be a true story. A senior Tory politician, calling on an elderly lady, was asked in for a glass of sherry. While waiting in the living room, he couldn't help noticing a photograph of himself taken with the then-leader of the Conservative Party, Harold McMillan. Both men were holding champagne glasses in one hand and a caviar snack in the other.

'I see you've noticed that photograph,' said the lady, bringing in the sherry. 'I keep it there to remind myself why I mustn't vote for you.'

GERALD KAUFMAN MP

You will recall that there were two General Elections in 1974. In the first, in February, I was canvassing in a street in my constituency called Shelford Avenue. I knocked at one door, and was answered by an elderly woman to whom I revealed my identity and explained my purpose.

'You only come round when it's election time,' she accused. I pointed out that I had tens of thousands of constituents and that it was physically impossible for me to call on them all regularly. Grumbling, she promised to vote for me.

In the October election one evening I found myself once again canvassing in Shelford Avenue and knocking at that same door. That same woman answered. She took one look at me and declared, 'It's you, is it? You're always round here.'

NICHOLAS BAKER MP

I was told that one lady I was going to call on had a complaint about the voting system. She was a very charming old lady who explained her difficulty to me.

'I do think it quite unfair that under our voting system we only have one vote,' she explained. I immediately assumed she was a supporter of proportional representation and started to explain some of the disadvantages of PR.

'No, no, you don't understand,' she said. 'I believe we should have enough votes to enable us to vote for every candidate if we want to. After all most parliamentary candidates are nice people and all the political parties have something to offer.'

COLIN MOYNIHAN MP (Cons)

As a former Political Advisor to Francis Pym, the then Secretary for Foreign and Commonwealth Affairs, my first campaign at the 1983 General Election in Lewisham East was dominated by the presence of many overseas journalists and Parliamentarians sent down by the Foreign Office to observe our campaign tactics.

A Belgian TV crew duly arrived one afternoon specifically requesting a visit of a traditional Labour stronghold. Taking them to one of the council estates, we spent an anguished two-and-a-half hours unsuccessfully trying to convert Labour voters. Frus-

'Living on her own, she loves a bit of a chat'

tration set in and the TV producer asked us if we could find some Tory supporters on whom to exercise our charms. This wasn't easy. However, in the heart of this inner London estate we found two elderly ladies willing to give an interview.

After a few very carefully worded questions by me, the producer suddenly butted in, asking the ladies in a strong Belgian accent, 'Well, what do you think of Michael Foot?', to which one in a noble cockney accent replied ' 'E's lost 'is marbles, mate!'

Both TV producer and cameraman were well on their way to Ostend as her companion finished explaining what his marbles were.

JOHN WARDEN (Political Editor, *Daily Express*)

Christopher Price was Labour MP for Lewisham West from 1974 until 1983.

It happened that a namesake, Henry Price, was Tory MP for the same seat from 1950 to 1964. That was a long time ago – but his memory still lingered in the minds of elderly Tory ladies. They told Price that yes, dear boy, they'd vote for him because 'they knew his father' and other suchlike reassurances.

He often wondered how much of his slender 900 majority consisted of unwitting Tory votes.

SIMON COOMBS MP

One of the problems which most canvassers have come across in their time is the awkward situation where the occupants of one house have been pasted on to two canvass cards, as a result of incorrect cutting up of the electoral register.

It so happened that on one occasion, I was the second person to canvass a small terraced house in my constituency on behalf of the Conservative Party on the same evening. On explaining who I was, I was informed by an elderly resident that she had indeed already been 'done'. I said I was terribly sorry for disturbing her evening and added, 'I am afraid there must have been some duplication of labour.'

'Oh no', she replied, 'duplication of Conservative.'

HUMFREY MALINS MP (Cons)

I was contesting Liverpool Toxteth in 1974, a safe Labour seat held by the legendary Dick Crawshaw. For the Conservatives, it was an act of faith. My parents drove from London to be on hand on polling day and my father was sent three miles across the City to pick up five elderly Tory ladies, some of whom weren't quite ready. It took him two hours. After he had delivered them all carefully to the polling station and chauffeured them safely back home, they turned to him and said:

'We have always admired you, Mr Crawshaw, and you know the Labour Party can always count on our votes.' My father was too heartsick to make a reply.

LORD WALLACE

When canvassing with a group of Young Socialists in Norwich, I heard some of them laughing and went over to find the cause. It appeared that a dear old lady, on being asked if she would vote Labour, said: 'I can't hear you very well. I must go and get my spectacles.'

GUY BARNETT MP

On election day a splendid, old Rolls Royce turned up at Labour Party headquarters in Dorset, offering to help. I did ask the chauffeur whether he was at the right place but he assured me he was. And he did a sterling job, driving many supporters to vote. The following day I called at the address he had given and was confronted by two elderly spinster ladies whom I thanked profusely for the use of their car. 'Not at all, Mr Barnett,' they said politely. 'Though we must tell you, if there had been a Communist standing we'd have offered the car to him.'

Which called to mind visions of the Communist candidate cruising round in state, painting the town red.

RONALD FRASER (activist)

In the 1955 election when the number of cars candidates could use taking voters to the polls was strictly limited, I was the Liberal standard bearer in West Aberdeenshire. I canvassed two charming elderly ladies living in a remote corner of Strathdon. Having established they were supporters, I asked if I could arrange for a car to run them to the polling-station which was a considerable distance away.

One of the ladies replied sweetly: 'Oh dear no, thanks. We're not well off and we're old so there's little we can do to further the Liberal cause. Several elections ago we decided that our most effective contribution would be to phone the Tory agent and organize for one of their cars to take us to cast our votes. We've done so ever since and we've never voted other than Liberal.'

DAVID AMESS MP

After attending an important service at a church in my constituency I was introduced to various 'worthies' outside the church, and in particular to one gentleman who proudly introduced me to his 98-year-old mother. I was left alone with her for a little while and racked my brains for something to say to such an elderly citizen. Visions of maundy money and big puffs at 100 candles flashed to mind, so I said that 'I very much looked forward to attending your 100th birthday in a couple of years' time.' There was a pause, and then the venerable one eyed me sternly.

'Well that's a wicked thing to say,' she said. 'Fancy wishing anyone to live to be 100.'

LORD MACKIE

When I was fighting the Caithness General Election in 1964, two lady supporters went to canvass an old lady of about 80 who came to the door smoking a pipe. They duly launched into a description of Liberal policies – which seemed to have no effect. So one of the ladies said: 'Anyhow, you should vote for George Mackie, he's the best man.'

Whereupon the old lady's eyes gleamed and seizing the canvasser's arm, she said: 'Hoo dae ye ken – have you tried him?'

LORD DIAMOND

In 1945 when I first contested the Blackley division of Manchester there was an area within the constituency known as Blackley Village, whose community was separated from its neighbours by tradition and by the physical contours of the land. Time seemed to have passed it by.

I canvassed the first house. In due course, after a good deal of shuffling and unlocking, a very old lady appeared and I went into my party piece, inviting her to vote for me. She listened carefully, but put her finger up to stop me.

'Sorry to interrupt you, love,' she said, 'but I always vote for Mr Gladstone.'

PAMELA HOWARTH (Tory activist)

Canvassing in the local Council elections in Harrow, I witnessed an old lady, taking a nap in her daughter's sitting room, waking up to find a man in the room with his trousers down.

It was the candidate, who'd been sent in there to inspect the bite he'd just received from the family dog.

JERRY HAYES MP

When I was canvassing during the 1983 General Election, a charming and matronly old lady told me that not only was she going to vote for me, but she would put up a poster in her window. At this point I was beaming with delight. I noticed that the lady had a pussy cat, so as all politicians are supposed to be animal lovers, I made a particular point of speaking to the old lady and stroking her cat at the same time.

Suddenly there was a most dreadful noise. I looked down and saw to my horror that the cat was being violently sick on my right shoe.

PAMELA HOWARTH (Tory activist)

Canvassing for the Council elections on a Bank Holiday, the dour lady was visibly relieved when the candidate fixed her faulty stopcock.

Earlier, she had told him categorically, that how she voted was a secret between her and the ballot box. But, as he left, she called after him: 'Ye shall judge them by their works.'

LIONEL EVANS (activist)

I knocked on a door in Leamington and it was opened by two elderly ladies. When I explained what I was there for, they smiled in a saintly way and one lady said, 'We don't vote.' The other added: 'On religious grounds.' I tried to persuade them of the error of their ways but they seemed adamant. 'We don't need to vote,' they told me, 'we've already got our Man.' And they looked Heavenwards. 'But what if he's not standing in this constituency?' I asked . . . to a door which had shut abruptly.

Postscript

. . . from ROBIN CORBETT MP

Oh, for the old happy days when politics really *were* politics . . . as this letter from the Shrewsbury Chronicle of November 12, 1774 illustrates. It is addressed by the sitting MP to constituents who wanted him to oppose the Excise Bill:

Gentlemen:

I received yours and am surprised at your insolence in troubling me about the Excise. You know what I very well know, that I bought you and by God I am determined to sell you. And I know, what perhaps you think I do not know, you are now selling yourselves to somebody else. And I know what you do not know, that I am buying another borough. May God's curse light on you all. May your houses be as open and common to all Excise Officers as your wives and daughters were to me when I stood for your rascally Corporation.

> *Yours*
>
> *Antony Henley MP*

. . . and from VAL HUDSON

I've just been told this allegedly true story:

An ex-MP, hungry for another seat, phoned the agent of a recently deceased sitting member. For some minutes he extolled the virtues of the departed MP, calling him 'not only a fine human being, but a wonderfully caring MP'.

At the end of the eulogy came the real reason for the call. 'Tell me,' asked the ex-MP, 'is there any chance I could take his place?'

The agent thought for a second. 'I don't know,' he said. 'I'll have to speak to the undertaker.'

Your Chance to be Famous!

We're looking for amusing, unusual or just plain daft electioneering stories for the next edition of *Can I Count On Your Support?* Please send as many stories as you like, to Robin Corbett MP, House of Commons, London SW1A 0AA. Please mark the envelope 'Canvassing Story'. Thank you for your help.